WORDS UNSPOKEN, THINGS UNSEEN

WORDS UNSPOKEN, THINGS UNSEEN

Joe Rodríguez

Copyright © 2014 by Joe Rodríguez.

Library of Congress Control Number:		2014907195
ISBN:	Hardcover	978-1-4990-0456-4
	Softcover	978-1-4990-0457-1
	eBook	978-1-4990-0455-7

All rights reserved. No part of this book may be reproduced or transmitted in any form or by any means, electronic or mechanical, including photocopying, recording, or by any information storage and retrieval system, without permission in writing from the copyright owner.

This is a work of fiction. Names, characters, places and incidents either are the product of the author's imagination or are used fictitiously, and any resemblance to any actual persons, living or dead, events, or locales is entirely coincidental.

This book was printed in the United States of America.

Rev. date: 05/28/2014

To order additional copies of this book, contact:
Xlibris LLC
1-888-795-4274
www.Xlibris.com
Orders@Xlibris.com
542676

1

*L*ORD GOD, APOSTLE *of children, shield this boy from his father. Keep Juanito safe in our shelter with us—away from Silvio's latest binge of repentance. Turn aside this haphazard pretender. No child should be baptized in a bar!*

"Silvio says he'll call the police," insists Guzmán at the rectory door. "Talk to him, Reverend Steve!"

The minister's head is bowed and his hands clasped. Guzmán lets him finish as he imagines the words:

In your name, our settlement welcomes the alien and orphan as you do in your gospel. Stretch out your hand. Redeem the boy's future. Otherwise, pride poison's hope. Do not misguide your servant, this blind man on the road.

"He wants his son now," Guzmán says. "The law's on his side."

"Damn the law," the pastor replies. "Silvio strands him in bars." But then the padre stares at his palms and offers, "Let me try patience."

"I'll take out the trash," mutters Guzmán, who's the shelter's handyman and the minister's assistant. He leaves by the fire exit, for Juanito's sake.

Outside an open window, teams of residents stand and listen, although they're assigned to help tidy the grounds before dinner.

Once Guzmán reaches the mission garden, the ex-boxer plucks a cabbage white butterfly from a row of sweet basil and squeezes his fist. Wiping away the glittery slime with some mulch, Guzmán surveys the run of pole beans and the mounds of squash, but then he glances back at the shouting.

Juanito sings in the choir, Guzmán mocks the slit sky. Shouldn't there be some break for him?

"A dispensation," he murmurs finally, recovering the term. "Cut the kid some slack. Call down some lightning." Guzmán feints with his jab like he once boxed in the ring under his fighting name, Molca. He worries about the punches costing his mind. Juanito's distracted also, with his father just out of jail.

The traffic beyond the men's and women's dormitories rumbles and honks. A car alarm blares as maritime clouds scrape overhead.

Guzmán turns to the tomato vines that teeter in a stiff breeze, swirling between the buildings. He butts a cobblestone against one redwood stake then the next and tests each trellis to make sure that they hold. The strikes numb his arm—the burred splinters don't register.

The wind shifts from the ocean.

He steps back and eyeballs his work. A few tomatoes have shaken loose from the blows. These he stacks for the kitchen. The soft mulch where they fell didn't split the skins.

A wrentit chirps close by while searching for bugs. *Providence eats sparrows*, Guzmán thinks, imagining Juanito crouching within earshot. *Keep your head down!*

And the boy's not the only one missing. Doc Reese has been absent the last three days because of cancer, which has spread through his body, not just his bones. *Dr. Manfred Saul Reese, MD, the captain of secrets, a blue-water sailor who took to sea with his ghosts.* Most people address him as Dr. Reese. The boxing team calls him Doc Manny. Only his friends use plain Manny.

Doc's father, Osmond "Ossie" Reese, also served in the navy, including World War II and Korea. Putting on a brave face was expected at home, especially for the next of kin. The enemy's watching and testing morale.

Molca was also taught to obey, no matter what, though only his cousins served in the military. "Do what I say, not as I do." That was his father's line. Molca didn't rebel. Instead he made fun of other kids for wearing the wrong clothes or speaking with a broken accent. This fault-finding carried over to opposing boxers, especially those that he branded low class, inferior.

Doc Reese asked him, "Why stir up trouble, kid, when boxing's a sport?"

"I'm not ashamed of who I am," Molca shot back. But some hard fights ended his taunts, which Manny counted to the good.

Manny resigned from the navy in the '80s-1982, wasn't it? That was long before he coached youngsters at the Settlement. Molca's seen some of Doc's files with newspaper clippings about secret weapon tests and military experiments, including some from the '50s. Manny, though, shrugs and says, "Don't ask. Don't tell." But he serves as an expert witness for veterans and civilians who were exposed to toxic agents and who are suing the government for medical care and compensation.

Whenever the court bailiffs deliver legal papers, they read Doc an advisory about the National Secrets Act. That Miranda-like warning about censoring what he says puts the old man on trial. His record of service doesn't count. He's guilty by association, lumped with protest groups opposing the government, which makes him an outlaw. And that stigma rattles Guzmán because he hails from a barrio named Shelltown that's under a freeway. He can't undo how the people there rose up to fight for a park instead of letting the city build a police station.

Recently, Molca enrolled at the university where he takes night classes three days a week. He rides public transit because he doesn't own a car. On the bus, he carries his birth certificate and identification card, just in case. Once Doc Manny came out and admitted to him, "I'm marked too. Not by my skin." Guzmán didn't know what to say. And now the old man's gone missing for the last three days.

"Move in to the shelter with us, Doc," Guzmán murmurs. *Don't leave your bones in the streets, Commander, just because I judged you wrong.* What he wants to tell Doc Reese is that some friends arrive late, though it's not all their fault. Quality is in the person, not the brand. And Molca's slow on the uptake.

The ex-boxer brings both fists to his chest as if taking an eight-count in the ring. Manny's been a boxer himself since his teens, and he was a finalist for the Olympic team. In the navy, Doc trained intramural squads for the fleet tournaments on his own time. Now, the military won't pay Manny's pension. His lawyer wants his fees up front, and how can Doc work when the cancer attacks the bone marrow? There's not enough red blood cells. Now his organs are failing.

You need tranfusions, Molca thinks, *and I'm in, carnal*. Let me help.

Guzmán turns to an Anaheim chile plant tipping from the weight of spear-point green peppers. A few wire twists secure the stem to the stake. His stomach growls from the scent, which reminds him that Juanito must be hungry too. The kid loves *chile relleños*. When the savory pods are at harvest, the Settlement serves the *relleños* fresh made, the cheese filling steamy and hot.

There will be no meal period if the city levels the place. A few votes on the district council pause the demolition. Doc and the minister talk to anyone who listens.

And Guzmán recalls how the the kids' boxing team turned into zombies in order to save the mission. **Save Our Hundred Beds,** their video urged, as they stalked the shelter's sidewalks in ragged formation.

Sidewalks Aren't Pillows, read the captions. Juanito posted the tube on the Internet, and the video went viral clocking thousands of hits. "The Young Dead," the team called themselves, and they fit right in at the comic convention downtown, along with the Flash and Wonder Woman. They welcomed attention.

The media picked up the story about the homeless and America's Finest City, which ate another mud pie for not taking care of its own.

Silvio showed up at the comic convention, though, ordered Juanito home and pushed Doc aside. "I know what you are, old man, Captain Queer, Almost Man. Rules stay in the ring."

"What do you know?" Doc Reese said, tapping his hat. "You're stuck up here."

Silvio slapped away the Panama.

With so many cameras around, Molca retrieved the elder's fine top and handed it back. He strolled over to Silvio with a soda cup and whispered, "This is for teeth, Loudmouth, yours get it!" All the while Molca kept smiling as if things were okay.

Good ol' dad, bendito 'apa, Molca muses in the mission garden about parents who don't make the grade. *Is the disease catching?* His own father never should have married, and his mother shouldn't have stayed. Some children never arrive. Is that so bad?

Wielding the cobblestone hammer like he was training with weights, Guzmán pounds a planting staves's blunt edge. He stretches his bad shoulder. Molca's three-year-old son, Tizoc, lives with the boy's mother, Inéz, and hides when Molca visits. Doubt is the boy's father, which tangles the relationship. Their DNA isn't a match. But whoever's the donor hasn't come forward. What are the kid's chances to thrive?

Out of a trance, Molca recalls that Silvio leaves the shelter through an alley, not by the front street. A bar's closer that way. *El jefe* buys drinks for the house while his family in Shelltown scrapes beans on tortillas.

Molca jogs over to a nearby security fence where a gnarled pomegranate tree overhangs the side lane. He fingers the keyring on his belt, the keys to the mission. Silvio wants his handyman's job, always has. To Silvio's mind, Molca's not the better man: *The minister plays favorites. So to get even, let the place burn. Toss a match!*

The ex-flyweight slides a rusted milk crate next to the chain-link perimeter that's backed with no-see tarp, steps up, and unlocks the gate, peering upwind and down. He turns his good eye to the light. Scrap paper skims the pocked broken glass; a scavenging dog tacks into the shadows.

Molca picks up a stray cobblestone from a pile of rubble. No one's come by yet—he cradles the love in his fist. An ambush is hard to do, especially with Doc and the boy on his mind. But Silvio deserves worse.

"Hey, brother," Reverend Steve sings out from behind him, "setting out the trash?" The padre tows up a green barrel crammed with plant clippings and weeds.

"Prop it open, my friend. Steady on." The pastor nods at the stone. "I tossed Silvio out," the preacher admits. "My temper got the best of me. We're a match there, Molca—God help us!"

Guzmán wedges the gate open with the rock as if recycling trash was his plan all along. "Jesus might come tomorrow, Padre!" The flyweight stands up and fakes the sign of the cross. "Sure he will, early . . . to set things right. Sort the wheat from the chaff. Meanwhile, no damage, no foul."

The preacher laughs as they scoot out the rubbish, though he shakes his head. Service to others anchors his faith, not passing judgment. Molca respects him for that. "Let's harvest those big boys," the minister weighs in, "and cook up a tub of sauce. Spaghetti brings a full house!"

Over a hundred mouths for each and every meal breakfast, lunch, and supper. Guzmán cracks his sore back and yawns. The homeless line up down the block. He keeps his good eye on the alley and recalls their hard luck stories, all sorts, from evictions to catastrophic medical bills. And that doesn't include the battered youngsters like Juanito. Early afternoons, the padre walks down the waiting line at the mission, person by person. Need decides who shelters that night. Someone has to choose.

And Guzmán recalls the two separate times that he stood in that queue and hoped for a meal and a bed. Twice he hit bottom and checked in to the shelter, unlike Doc who would die rather than accept charity, especially a military funeral. Guzmán's first time at the mission was at sixteen, right out of reform school, Youth Authority. Doc Reese was his court-appointed guardian (there's a story), and Guzmán rebelled against his discipline, including being enrolled in Catholic school. Guzmán ran off and slept in canyons with the coyotes, until he started howling back at them.

Uncanny that howling, that wail after dark—echoing out there and a few feet away, close and far at the same time. He felt double. Split off, stuck. Isolation beat him, as if hybrid coywolves were circling round. He slunk back to the mission where Doc staffed the volunteer clinic three days a week. No white flag was more plain than his showing up.

The second time Guzmán queued up at the shelter was at twenty-two, after his busted eye gave out, and his ring days were over. He was a loser, ordinary, the generic brand X—so everyone said, though not to his face. Once he had been a contender, ranked at the top of ring magazines. Suddenly, pawnshops owned the trophies, and he was nobody. He turned his back on his job at the shelter, didn't work out at the gym, and lost track of his few friends. Try as he might, he couldn't stop the binges. There were times he came to and forgot how he got there.

One night, he woke up in an alley somewhere, cold and stiff. People get shot in the wrong neighborhood, so he tried to stand up and git. Couldn't budge, though, not a muscle. Nothing. He could feel his legs, but they wouldn't obey like being knocked loopy from a punch. He wet his lips to raise a squawk, in case someone might hear. Zero again. Lying flat made music play in his mind, *"Red red wine, go to my head, make me forget."*

Something must have popped in his brain from the punches and booze. *Shut up with the mind games, fool,* he told himself, *muévete.* But when he tried to stand, a different song started up, *Whiskey river, take my mind.*

The moon creaked overhead, then went blank. When he came to, dawn howled like jungle birds auditioning for Tarzan movies. No more booze, he swore, never again. Too many head shots, no anesthesia required to put him under the carpet. He stumbled to his feet and let the blood settle so he could walk. That's when he realized the zoo's over there, to the north. Cages are what you're hearing. Which means Balboa Park's close, the city's in the other direction. His head cleared enough so that he could navigate the streets downtown.

Hours later, he guessed, after arriving at the mission, he stood in single file with the other castaways, wrinkled and stale from his binge the previous night. The padre recognized him, however, though Molca hid his scarred knuckles and wrists.

"Welcome," the pastor said, clapping Molca's shoulder, "You dropped out of sight. We were worried. Can you do with a meal?"

And Molca glanced around at the other lean faces. "We all can make weight," he said, shamed as he was for just disappearing without notice. "Bring on the fatted calf." Molca juked a few steps like he was sparring for money, despite his baggy rummaged threads. He was being rescued. Be grateful! The padre was fifteen years his senior and had seen worse than a washed-up punk.

"Any chance for my old handyman's job?" he asked pastor Bentham, holding out his mitts. "You know I'm good with these."

Guzmán's jarred back to the present, right then. In the alley behind the mission, the reverend slides a trash barrel, hard. Guzmán makes the stop and pivots at the ready. Something's coming.

"*Oye*, it's the Lone Ranger and Tonto." Silvio Ron Téllez sneers from the shadows and stumbles up to them. "I'll be back for my boy," he belches. "You're responsible! The kid spends all his time here."

"Think you're so holy?" Silvio tugs at Steve's beard. "Juanito's young, doesn't know better."

The pastor flushes red but lets the insult go.

"I'll be back with the sheriff," Silvio repeats in the alley. "You're no better than me. No better than that loser." Silvio stabs a thumb at Molca.

"The city wants you out, reverend!" Silvio taunts his better. "Your reputation's shot. All that bad publicity! Your messy divorce included. Kind to strangers, bad for your wife! A video saved your ass, some stupid freak show on the Internet. You put those kids up to it."

"More slander, *vendido*," Molca steps in. "Who's paying for gossip, you sellout?"

"You going to hurt me, halfbreed?" Silvio cackles, "to protect Saint *Esteban* here. Where's the ladder, *tonto*," he jabs in Spanish. "Grow up!"

Just then the preacher taps Molca's shoulder.

"Make him heel, Padre!" Silvio smooches his mouth as if calling a mutt. Silvio turns to the pastor, "Take care of the dwarf!"

"Flyweight," Guzmán shoots back, "five-five, one hundred and twelve. Perfect size for your mother." He waggles his tongue.

Before Silvio tries a sucker punch, the preacher steps between them, although Guzmán's hoping the drunk throws first. He's ready.

"Juanito needs a father," the minister urges. "Come back when you're sober!"

"You don't pay for my beer!" Silvio spits in the dirt. "The city wants this property, and you got enemies! I'll report a kidnapping! They'll shut this swamp down."

"Not looking for trouble," Steve tells him. "Take this for bus fare. You go on home. All of us want what's best for your son."

As Silvio straightens his collar and eyes the money, Molca picks up the milk crate and steps through the fence.

Silvio snatches the bill and stuffs it in his pocket. "I'll be back with the cops!"

Once the preacher pulls the gate closed and snaps the lock, he walks to the garden. He stoops in the vines and harvests the ripe Brandywines one at a time.

"'Lead us not into temptation,'" Guzmán jests with the downcast man. But the minister doesn't laugh. Guzmán buffs a plump tomato and takes a bite. "Sainthood ain't easy, my friend. Ideals get tangled with people."

"Jesus sets the example," murmurs the preacher. "He was a Knight of the Ordinary."

"Hey, you're no Second Coming," Guzmán guffaws, trying to buck him up, "but you can cook. Wednesdays—it's pasta with Chef Steve!"

"And don't mind me," Molca says. "I've enrolled in college to reinvent myself." Then like a ring announcer he intones, "In this corner, meet our former contender, sporting two divorces and a kid."

"Do not fear, only believe," the minister offers from the Bible.

Guzmán sights down the rows, holding the half-eaten globe. "Juanito runs away because Silvio's out of jail," he reminds the pastor. "And the drunk's plastered in public again." So who cares? Not the chamber of commerce. Not the Alliance of Churches. Even the state university prefers real estate to teaching. All of them are a business. Professor Lyle Carson, the minister's nemesis from the college, chairs the Downtown Redevelopment Committee.

"All those smart people," Molca turns to the preacher. "Charles Darwin is king, the great evolutionist."

Molca takes the last bite of the Brandywine and wipes his mouth. When you bed down on sidewalks, Darwin's notion of "the survival of the fittest" hits close to home. The fault you're down and out has to be your own.

In his defense, Guzmán can't bring into evidence the famous anthropology Professor John Peabody Harrington, PhD, to argue about why some people go extinct and others don't. History blindsided whole tribes of Native Americans like a runaway train. A cache of Harrington's research is hidden right here at the shelter detailing their demise when the West was won. But that mother lode is Rhoda Bart's secret, hidden in her lab. Harrington's documents, which have been lost for a hundred years maybe, preserve the languages of the disappeared American Indians. Guzmán, though, has a key to Rhoda's room and time to roam through and play the spy.

Plus, Rhoda's uncovered personal letters from Harrington to his wife Carobeth Laird from the 1920s when Carobeth was filing for a divorce.

Guzmán's read them on the sly—more than a few times, in fact. Nobody suspects what Rhoda's found, or what they're worth. That one find is worth plenty, the notoriety included, because of how the letters turned up. Harrington never mailed them. Read and understand why!

Enough of that maundering, punchie, Molca stops himself. Juanito comes first, *pendejo. Ya basta* with your rope-a-dope mental games.

Shelter residents are busy nearby tending the garden, cleaning up the place. Guzmán and the padre stay by themselves, hoeing weeds and raking mulch while keeping an eye out for the boy or his father, Silvio. Close by the knoll run Rhoda's archeology trenches, perfect for hiding. And at the base of the rise across from the plants is a concrete-lined caisson deep as a grave, a cofferdam built as a foundation for a memorial fountain. The inspiration is a sculpture welded from metal where water cascades. Doc Manny made a sizeable donation so that the birds could drink.

For Guzmán, the fountain reminds him that here's a chance to to do right by his coach. Sometimes it takes years to sort out what matters. *I won't let the military bury the commander. Not the way they forced him out. When the maestro passes away from cancer, he will have a headstone just as he wants.*

What inspires Guzmán is the shelter garden growing out of cement.

Because of Dr. Reese, fresh vegetables replaced a broken-down courtyard that was cracked and busted up, an eyesore for years. That dead space was used for offstreet storage and parking at the mission. Manny and Juanito used to spread birdseed there, and they did for several seasons. That's their hobby, watching birds. Manny and the kid counted the finches, wrens, or whatever flies in. And some of the millet that they cast for the strays sprouted from the cracks in the decrepit antique. The grassy tufts blossomed into seed.

A flock of lesser goldfinches appeared to gorge on the bounty twenty-two or so, parakeet-size, smaller, perching on the stalks, twittering and wild. Juanito recorded the songs on the minister's cell phone.

Bright wings flashed everywhere.

Which lifted spirits, the pastor's especially, what with managing a shelter that the city wants out. Admire those feathers! Hear the music! All that color from a slab of busted cement! The minister took the sign to heart.

Doc Reese and the pastor wondered, *Why not plant a garden instead of letting weeds grow? Raise vegetables for the kitchen!*

Molca stretches his back among the furrows, recalling the project: The four of us rented a jackhammer, a compressed air drill that weighs sixty-five pounds. To plant fresh greens like kale, chard and such, we all must bust through the concrete first—the padre, Doc, the boy, and me. Hardpan clay came in the next layer down.

Shovels and picks were locked in the toolshed, but hand tools don't cut it. Demolishing concrete demands hammered steel! Over one long weekend and hours at a stretch, they peeled away the brittle courtyard pavement with truckloads of rubble. Doc Manny and the boy teamed up and used a stray grocery cart. The pastor and Guzmán pushed wheelbarrows.

After that marathon clear-and-haul, they mixed in acres of mulch to break down the dirt and let the worms have a go. By that point, Doc Manny taped their blisters. They measured out the furrows and heaped up mounds of loam, then planted various crops according to the kitchen's menu.

Once the table greens came in—lettuce and spinach and then the okra and squash and tomatillos. Molca and Doc didn't have to cadge produce as often from grocers and supermarkets, which was okay for those two. It wasn't just about begging for charity or saving money. A fresh-picked meal tastes special.

Close by the new garden, however, interred under the uncapped soil, they dug up relics: a chipped buckle from a Union soldier; further down, an empty whisky bottle branded Old Scout and coins dating from around the California Gold Rush; lower still, broken crockery that had sailed round the Horn of South America, maybe in clipper ships.

That's when the padre called in Professor Rhoda Bart from the university to examine the artifacts. She's a licensed archeologist, just like John Peabody Harrington.

Down deep in the earth, she excavated buttons from a Mexican cavalry uniform. In a lower deposit, she retrieved a rusted scraper for tanning hides—property of Spanish friars from around the 1790s, probably. Shards of tribal pottery were strewn beneath, with designs from different eras.

One weekend, the professor's archeology students unearthed a killed mortar and pestle: a hole chiseled through the stone bowl, the head of the pestle cracked in pieces, perhaps to free the implement's power and not anger the spirits. That find dated from before the Spanish conquest according to a crosstown university's isotope dating machines. Which invited a conjecture. Prehistoric Indians might have used that very *molcahete*, or grinding stone, to prepare sacred Jimson root as a spirit guide to the shadow world. Some *indios* still do today.

Guzmán took the reminder of his nickname Molca, the grinding stone, as a sign of good luck, which made the professor grin. There was a first. So he kept pressing the advantage.

Gesturing at his nappy hair and Geronimo nose, he joked, "All this stuff you've dug up. It's personal. My roots are *mestizo*, from many strands. I'm making a comeback not as one thing or the other."

"A melting pot," she answered. "My family's German and Scotch-Irish."

"Try American Indian, Africa, and Europe," he countered. "Mix and match." And he scraped the soil not sure what that meant about being neither black or white, and yet both. He's enrolled at the university to reinvent himself.

Juanito's new country too, Molca thinks, despite the fact that Silvio who claims pureblood Spanish brands his son, "*morenito*, the dark one." *There's my mission*, Molca muses. *Not X or Y, but all of the above, including your own kid with Inéz*, he thinks to himself.

And back at the mission garden standing watch for Juanito, Molca smells the sea wind gusting from the bay. *What about the first sailing ships back in the 1500s?* he wonders, the Spanish galleons. I was a sailor then, maybe a soldier at the end of my rope, a fugitive likely. A ship is an island, and each voyage is a first. The masts were tall as trees with spars for branches. When the lookout cried, "land ho," I stared at the tribes on the shore. There I was too.

Did the *indios* foresee the forced baptisms and imported epidemics? The measles took me along with a thousand people, the small pox and mumps also.

Guzmán recalls that Harrington recovered dead tribal languages, which modern descendents are relearning to speak. What's salvage and worth preserving? Molca wonders, What's to keep? Rhoda has science. The padre has the Bible. The Olympics inspired Doc.

As for me? To discover a new land, I need a new way to dream.

Every year, Molca's barrio, named Shelltown, which is close by the city, celebrates the day of the dead for All Souls' Day, around Halloween. Juanito's not afraid of the skeletons. But with the devil masks, yes.

Strange how a ghost hijacked Rhoda—sorry for the familiarity, Professor Bart. She mines the ghost of John Peabody Harrington. Salvaging near-extinct Indians was the man's obsession. In the early 1900s, he tracked down the last survivors of native tribes. These "informants," the final handful who spoke their ancestral dialects, were his reason for living—these interviews meant life or death.

Stranger still is how the scientist's last stand became those secret letters to his then-wife Carobeth Laird, letters that he never mailed.

Molca's spied on Harrington's stuff, though he feels like a Peeping Tom. Carobeth shacked up with a blacksmith named George Laird while she and Harrington were married. But from day one, Harrington was wed to his fieldwork, so he abandoned her for months at a time even when she was pregnant with their only child, a daughter they named Awona.

Maybe some people are deaf in the heart.

Carobeth finally had enough.

And yet sad those dead letters are, pathetic, begging Carobeth to stay in the marriage and halt the divorce. They weren't even mailed. He tried to save the Indians, and all the while he's losing himself? Brilliant in the lab, but absent elsewhere.

Rhoda believes that Harrington's mildewed envelopes are her secret, Guzmán muses. And Guzmán has reason for not telling her different—that he's read them, in fact. Harrington is too important to peddle for profit since he's kin, not by blood, necessarily, but imagination. We inherit mutiple legacies. They reflect us. To be is a chorus not one thing or another, not just one culture to the exclusion of another. A person's identity is patched like a quilt. There's reason to hope for a future—at least to Molca's mind.

The ex-boxer grew up hearing that his ancestry is mixed. That the past isn't one-sided. We start from scratch each generation and reinvent ourselves. People, though, don't put much stock in a handyman, a busted-up ex-pug. Harrington's artifacts and notes are priceless if Rhoda shows why. Although Harrington has the credentials, he's an underdog too. A compulsive hoarder obsessed with preserving the lifeways of native people, he was estranged from his contemporaries and unwilling to share his ideas.

And in his mind's eye, Molca pictures Professor Bart at the shelter teaching Juanito how to unbury the past from the ground, for better or worse.

"Hey, Short Round, you back in school," Guzmán sings out as Rhoda and the boy scrape away earth bit by bit near the future fountain.

A pottery shard or musket ball can hide underfoot just a few steps away from the cofferdam, right there.

And Juanito whoops and windmills his arms, he's so revved. Discovery is his.

Right now, Juanito's hunkered down close by the garden, probably. Where else is safe?

And Molca recalls the time when suburb fly-by's flocked to the Settlement, itching to volunteer and get their hands dirty with Rhoda's digging. The local paper ran a Sunday series about how archeology unburies history, layer by layer. As a result of the coverage, contributions increased—which was good. People flocked to the place and picked up a trowel.

But once the publicity faded, there went the visitors interested in our mongrel roots—those grudging affinities that provoke transformation. The professor, though, has staying power for mysteries, not a moth's mind for fads. With crowds or not, she digs up old settlements and recovers what people build and wear and throw away. Patterns emerge about groups, such as how they mark men and women as male and female. These ancient ways of thinking she calls "archogenics." Yet she's optimistic about change: To know a name implies that it can be rephrased, changed if need be.

Just weeks ago, a tribal elder prayed at the dig, conducted a ceremony to honor the ancestors. On the shaman's own land, miles away, the holy man uses Jimsonweed for "seeing" the spirit world. One special power of the Jimson plant, the native *toloache*, turns boys into men at an initiation ceremony called a "vision quest."

Juanito, though, needs more than a coming-of-age ritual, Molca reasons. The kid's mestizo and has to bridge worlds, which is hard. A ship in a bottle has no horizon. Monotony's a boneyard.

"The Settlement," Guzmán murmurs, "a lifeline for misfits, outlaws, and folk down on their luck. A flop for the night, plus a shower and toothbrush. Hot steam clouds the glass. Hit bottom, though, and mirrors scare you. Which never changes, whether fortune ever finds you or not."

Take heart, though, from kindred spirits, four of us: a physician, a minister, a professor, and me.

2

RHODA'S BREATH CATCHES as an ambulance speeds past the mission. Silvio's yelling in the rectory. He wants his son. Juanito's run away again. The last time he hid in the toolshed—the time before that, in the plants.

She buries a sheaf of files in a desk drawer and hurries out the door of her lab.

No weapons are permitted at the shelter which is a policy at the college too where last spring, three professors were shot dead.

The siren dopplers away.

Outside, a team of new residents patrol for litter which is their assignment before dinner. On her way to Steve's office, the commotion ceases.

By the time she arrives at the threshold, no one answers. She knocks twice and tries again. Then she tests the lock to the manse and enters.

Though the lights are on, the desk chair is pulled back. Nothing else is disturbed. She steps inside and calls.

The sun-bleached ecru curtains were Regina's choice when she and Steve married. Regina's missing photos float on the walls. Steve keeps promising to paint the shadows.

At least the pastor and Rhoda are doubles that way, with failed marriages. If the past haunts our choices, shouldn't regrets make us wiser?

Rhoda rubs her temples again: *Tell him what you discovered! Tell Steve about the Harrington find. For whose good, though?* she wonders. *Not for the shelter, not for the residents.*

By law, the pastor must disclose the smallest artifact at the dig, anything with archeological value. Any document or scrap of paper counts. Especially a trove from John Peabody Harrington, if her discovery is Harrington's, in fact. To be fair, proof hasn't been met. But doubt is the way she lives now, and not just because of the self-fulfilling prophecy. Steve's a man of faith, she's a scholar. Splitting the difference isn't possible.

No, she hasn't told the pastor everything. He assumes that there's a meeting of minds about trust. He's never demanded an inventory. Rhoda, however, considers more than the Commandments.

Again, she checks the window.

Outside, the siren's gone, for now.

Her task for the present is locating, recording, and dating archeological finds. That's why she searches for old records, any document with provenance, any item that fixes a chronology of who lived here and when. Such inquiry helps assign dates when nothing's official. She's turned over a bill of lading from 1867 when the first hotel was built; receipts from 1900s when the place was a warehouse; newsprint from the '20s when it was converted to a store. Smudged receipts, ancient ledgers, even a few black-and-white photos. But she hasn't handed over everything. Perhaps that's why she can't rest? What's sleep and what's death?

She feels unmoored in time, always arriving, which is fitting, maybe. She's a scholar, a teacher, even one of the Settlement volunteers, it feels like. Her sense of self seems negotiable—many voices, many strands. Maybe from all the digging, all the layers of history and habitation.

Rhoda walks to the rectory door and calls for the minister one last time. She leaves on the lights as she found them.

Outside, on a sliver of lawn, two women chase down a scrap of newsprint. One of them carries a garbage bag. The other clutches her jacket as if the zipper's broken.

A knoll nearby overlooks the mission grounds, and Rhoda heads for that lookout. As a passenger jet roars overhead, descends for a landing at the airport, the residents' children sing in the daycare center. The older ones are bused to school.

Where is the boy?

Juanito's home is in Shelltown nearby, where he attends Franklin Elementary. More days than not though, he stows away here instead of returning home. On the weekends, he never misses Rhoda's projects. Her anthropology students put their protégé to work, including recording the artifacts on the computer. Charting the dig in 3D fascinates him. Aerial views of the site swoop like a bird. He's good at the keys, a prodigy, in fact. Like his sister Serafina, he's gifted in science. Like her so much stands in the way of success.

And she recalls how Juanito wriggles through dusty crawl spaces and vents, explores walled off passageways. Anything old is the lure—tin cans and glass bottles, rusty tools and the like—scrap and rubbish. To him, boxes crammed with strange notebooks and illegible journals are for her. Real booty comes in pirate chests, as in *Treasure Island*.

Rhoda never planned on children—life is tangled enough. Strange how these waifs found her anyway despite her lone habit of mind. Her mother named her for a heroine who dies from poverty, unable to earn a living wage. Thelma was determined that Rhoda stand on her own, which helps account for her independence. Maybe the Settlement girls are drawn to her zest for archeology and come to see what she finds, the shells and broken plates, a comb and other personal items. The boys want to climb down in the trenches and dig. All of them skip away after a short while because nothing happens mostly.

Except for the boy Juanito, her self-appointed assistant, sporting the university sweatshirt that she gave him like a trophy. *Two Years before the Mast* is a favorite book, and waiting knits his life.

Rhoda kneads her temples again. The crushing insomnia is back—the Gray Shroud. Just as she's able to sleep without pills, a dead man robs her rest. Who can she tell, though, when no good will come.

From under a shaded kiosk on the knoll, Rhoda surveys her handiwork, a series of trenches that she plots on a grid. Each unburied artifact is mapped and photographed *in situ*.

A Harrington poem leaps to mind: "Give not the yawning graves their plunder; Save, save the lore, for future ages' joy."

She alone keeps that secret.

Poetry was his hobby, but above all, dead languages came first. He mailed off boxcars of research to the Bureau of Ethnic Affairs in Washington, DC., where they were stored in bulk. Even today, Harrington's work remains unpacked. Nonetheless, the city, the federal government, and especially her university will all stake a claim to her find, once she speaks up. And paying lawyers to sort out possession will rob a hundred people of food and a bed.

The shelter survives month to month. How long can she hide the truth? Dr. Reese has an inkling that something's up, but Rhoda trusts his silence. Many residents hold on day to day, like her mom. Like Thelma, Doc's in chemotherapy too. And people in the same boat use their first names.

The Settlement's managing right now. But tomorrow? The day after?

Rhoda hasn't mentioned to her mom that Doc's missing. But Thelma knows. What does it mean to hope against hope? Rhoda wonders. To pile up a levee and wait for high tide.

This early morning, the chair of her department, Professor Ernst "Ernie" Spiller, telephoned. "Good morning, Rhoda," Professor Spiller announced. "Fine day to be in the field. Wish I was back."

She recognized that academic pose, mannered, resonant—a fluent sham. Don't smell his breath.

"I just sent the latest tally for our fund-raiser," announced Ernie. "Donations are right on target. That dig of yours is wonderful publicity. Our campus museum is featuring the artifacts. Anything new to report?"

Rhoda tried to stay matter-of-fact, although she hadn't had her coffee yet. "Nothing so far," she ventured. "There's a book to write . . ."

"If only knowledge paid for itself," her chair interrupted. "Right now, the college needs endowments.

"Contact my office if you uncover anything new," he insisted. "Even if you haven't run all the tests. The alumni newsletter goes out this week. Planned Giving is leading the charge." And the chair hurried his goodbye and left, although usually he's a genial plantation owner.

Next to Rhoda's phone on her desk is a copy of *Encounter with an Angry God,* which her ex-husband Lyle Carson just mailed with a note. "I'm applying for tenure and promotion again! Hope all is well." He includes his business card: *Assistant Professor Lyle Carson, Department of Anthropology, Acting Vice President for Planned Giving.*

A few years ago, she might have panicked. Does Lyle know? Is that why he sent her Harrington's biography? Fund-raising, however, is Lyle's new make-or-break job, and Harrington once taught for the college. There's a pitch for alma mater. Daggers already would be out if Lyle suspected her find. Lyle and she were colleagues once, now he's no friend. Sharing professions doesn't ensure a bond, certainly not a mate.

Without trust, whatever she chooses to do has to be on solid footing. What if the letters are fakes? Rhoda retested the null hypothesis, the premise that the mystery correspondence isn't Harrington's. Her strategy was to determine whether or not the pouch containing the mildewed trove comes from the Karuk tribe. This culture is featured in the linguist's famous monograph on native tobacco. And the weaving was indisputable, plus the basket still carries that scent. She couldn't prove the lie.

Similar Karuk baskets are on display at the campus museum because Harrington's daughter bequeathed a collection of woven goods to the college. Rhoda examined the lot, which took hours. No matter how she tried to deny the evidence, one conclusion stuck. The provenance is clear.

And that bundle is in her room.

But on campus, among the basket collection, as she matched one item against another, her fingers felt stiff and cold. She compared the containers to the one back at the Settlement, the pouch near her desk. She kept reminding herself that she was at the university. The college museum's lights were kept low, so she took care studying the construction of the craftwork, the material, identified the decoration, even the dyes. She went item by item, handling each piece as if it might break.

The gallery interns who retrieved the Harrington specimens whispered behind their hands. *Why is there no term for a cuckolded wife?* she wondered. Where on campus can she go without the glances? Even graduate students stare.

On the museum shelves, several pieces were tagged in Harrington's distinct handwriting, brief inscriptions with the tribal affiliation and function: Yurok storage basket, Hupa burden basket, and the like. She took pictures with her cell phone. Dwelling too long on one piece or another might arouse suspicion. Besides, she was exhausted. Doubt and uncertainty are good for experiments, not a pillow.

A close-up was in her phone-camera when Lyle's replacement at the university gallery appeared straightening his tie. Professor Timothy Pemberton was now the director of the campus museum. "Professor Bart, Rhoda, I wish you had called."

"Just catching up on some research, Tim," she replied to the formality. "The Settlement . . . ," she offered and stopped. Something was cooking.

He tugged at his sleeves and smiled.

"What artistry," she held out a decorative twining of sumac root and bear grass.

He glanced away at the shelf.

"How's your study on the Chumash coming?" she asked as she handed back the art. "I see that you're quoted in Sunday's edition of the *Times*, the feature on tribal descendants today recovering their culture from studying Harrington's notes."

"Fine, fine," Tim stammered. And that was all.

She packed up her scribbling and retrieved her shawl.

The quiet bristled like an ambush as Tim escorted her outside the campus gallery. With the coast clear, the first thing he'd do is call Lyle, who had been transferred to the administration.

Now that Lyle works for the Office of Planned Giving, he chairs a committee of local stakeholders that champions the stadium downtown.

The university has several projects in the inner city, including tracking returning veterans and counting the homeless. And as for why an assistant professor heads the stadium committee, no one else wants the job. The previous chair was forced out. The college offered Lyle as an interim replacement, and he accepted the nomination to save his career. Lyle's recent book on Native American culture offended some donors from local tribes. He either mends fences or moves on. Far afield to be exact.

"I'm applying for promotion and tenure," read Lyle's note to Rhoda. "Hope all is well."

Back at the shelter, a mockingbird's song rattles a tree.

Lyle never loved her—she deluded herself. Lyle's PhD dissertation in anthropology examines whether early people migrated in boats to Australia. Her doctorate in the same field pursues the conjunction of writing and pottery in Classical Mayan culture. Both of them were trained to suspend belief in a lab and follow the data wherever it led. But doubt is not a free pass and gives no license to cheat. He had lied for convenience.

What Rhoda lost was her trust in a marriage of minds. A person is never sure of the world. What couple enjoys better luck with each other?

Rhoda does know this: Carobeth Laird was Harrington's student in 1916. After a ragged courtship, they married.

During one rare interlude in *Encounter with an Angry God*, the couple travels to Santa Ynez where they throw off their clothes and wander the wild hills like "the natives of yore." Harrington even takes a day off to catalog the names of local plants, because Carobeth wants to learn about native medicine. Ever the scholar, nonetheless, he justifies their romp as an experiment.

Science is all too human; Harrington is proof. Yet he's an easy target. Who doesn't mistake conviction for truth?

When Carobeth meets George Laird on an Indian reservation, she compares his gaze to the thrust of a phallus—but only in her tell-all book. Harrington seems oblivious that the marriage is doomed. He delegates her to interview Laird, one of the last of his Chemehuevi tribe that speaks the ancestral dialect. And then he leaves to pursue another informant.

Their three-ring circus begins, although Carobeth and Laird shadow dance at first. George Laird's father is of Scotch ancestry; his mother is Chemehuevi. He's smitten with Carobeth (her roots might include the Iroquois nation, although she's officially white). She wants a family, as does Laird. Harrington's a taxidermist of language, and notating speech leaves no time for children. And yet ancient dialects bring the three together as they compile spoken sounds into careful notes. Heartache, nonetheless, revolves around words, because we speak to what we assume is given and miss each other. Their ménage a trois shares a coffin.

Scant miles away from the shelter rises a mountain once held sacred by the first people in the Americas. Now, it's a hiking path. A reconstructed circle of rocks on a ledge tracks the sun's passage, like a sundial. If the anthropology's correct, whole villages kept rhythm by clocks such as this. Bonfires lit the winter solstice when the shadows aligned on the shortest day. The summer equinox signaled the moment to harvest and plant.

Rhoda has studied prehistoric calendars in different parts of the world, not just the Southwest but in Asia, Europe, and Africa. Which generation far back realized that the sun and the moon herald the seasons? The imagination engraves time on stone with light and shadow. The Chaco Canyon Sun Dagger and Stonehenge are among the earliest metaphors. These rock structures write in the air, although ink and paper are far in the future. No backward sort maps time on stone, transforms the space around us into a clock, nature into symbols. Mortality woke through them.

And Rhoda marvels that a master linguist such as Harrington, a genius with perfect pitch, preserves the voices of the ancestors while rarely minding Carobeth. The grave means not being able to think, which terrifies him. And he's obsessed with language, although he doesn't share much. Perhaps listening to others distracted him. He lost his focus. Life is too raw to digest wholly.

And yet, don't we have to unthink who we are to hear the past? And letting go of the self is a sort of death that needs practice. Yet Harrington appears deaf in the heart, estranged from his feelings and suspicious of others. How then could he value different cultures?

Or is questioning language just his thought experiment confined to the lab? Silencing the self is an exercise only. Nothing sensitive leaves the premises.

Where's the boy? she wakes with a start. The light's falling.

3

*H*UNGRY WINGS CIRCLE *the square patch of sky, a soaring bright falcon ready to pounce on the pigeons. The wings swoop in and out, in and out of the blue window of light as the breeze combs the feathers.*

For a moment, the boy himself is high up riding the gyre, banking in the wind. *Home is the air, free and alone.*

Finally, the silent tips soar out of view from inside the underground box, the boy's hiding place, the cofferdam hull, which waits for Doc Manny's fountain to be installed. Juanito wets his lips, but there's no water. When he glances up, the falcon disappears out of sight not because of the make-believe owl that's nailed to the toolshed to scare away pests. That faded old copy has no power to harm.

The boy's seen the proof in the garden!

Down in the furrows one day without warning, a house sparrow blew up in a puff of feathers. "Whoa," *I jumped.* Before I could breathe, yellow blinking eyes carried off the flat balloon. Nothing was left but feathers that stuck to the dirt, as I searched underfoot. Some white puffy down stuck to red bits of meat. All was quiet, except for the streets.

I sit against the rough scrapey walls of the concrete box, press my back hard so that I'm not hungry. The kitchen's baking sourdough bread.

Even seated low in this cement coffin, I hear the pigeons flap and coo as they gobble the birdseed set out for the garden finches and sparrows and wrens. The plastic ghost owl doesn't scare any of them. Even the jumpy flock of wild Amazon parrots that crack open the fat sunflowers.

The pigeons' spiny beaks peck rat-a-tat as they crowd the feeders set up high from the alley cats. Some scratch for spilled grains on the concrete apron, which sounds like mice scrabbling behind walls late at night, when I close my eyes.

I toss gravel at the loud rat-birds—that's what Doc Manny calls the sheeny pecker-bills, street seagulls. *Doc Manny's a sailor who crossed the seas, so far over the ocean there are only waves and stars. Late nights the*

Milky Way shows overhead, not like a city that blocks the sky. Far over the water, shooting stars crisscross the dark.

I tell the other kids that my father Silvio Ron Téllez is a sailor too, which is why he disappears like sails in the ocean. *Boats at the horizon drop off the edge of the earth, just like my father. At least late night when he doesn't come home, there's no commotion—the house can rest.*

The emptiness shivers again in this square concrete hole by the garden, like under the classroom floor where I hide at the school. My ship is the silence. The darkness is my friend.

4

IN THE MISSION garden, as the pastor and Guzmán hunt for the last ripe tomatoes tucked in the vines, it's Guzmán who notices Rhoda standing beneath a tree-shaded pergola on the knoll. He tries to read her expression, but she's too far away. Rhoda's worried about the boy too, he guesses. As well as Doc Manny.

"*Hola, Profe,* come for some air. How about some color?" Guzmán dances up the brick pavers, half bobbing and weaving, half strutting. He tips his fedora to a few diehard smokers in the light-up area, a snappy canvas model fit for indoors or out. Manny the Hat gave it for luck.

"Hello, Mr. G.," Rhoda greets Molca, although she's staring over his shoulder at the padre who shades his brow and waves.

Guzmán takes Rhoda's shot to the chest and pivots out of the way, mindful that the roll-your-own set is watching. King David has the professor's attention, not the boxer. That image leaps from the Bible when a ruler goes after a soldier's wife. So, Uriah, he mocks himself as if he were the cuckold, go back to your corner and spit in the bucket. This round's a bust too. Where's Doc Manny when you're pinned on the ropes and need help?

Guzmán, though, forces a smile although the day's been a bust. Rhoda wouldn't stop to talk. And Silvio just mocked him in the alley while the preacher kept the peace and held Molca back.

Ah, the preacher, his boss, and his friend. *But ask Molca why he's loyal, and he'd answer: On a dare, damn him. Maybe the pastor is the better man?*

Guzmán fans at the cigarette smoke as if he's corraling an addiction, which draws a laugh from the Bull Durham claque that's relaxing in the shade. And as Rhoda heads for the garden, Guzmán creases his good-luck hat so that no one can see the horns.

The apostle and the professor, he thinks to himself—two bookends pretending to be opposites. But difference depends on who's watching. Both of them live in the head.

Rhoda reaches the rows of pole beans and the mounds of multicolored squash planted beside eggplant fruiting in a palette of hues spanning ivory to aubergine. The rose sun is disappearing behind fiery skyscrapers downtown, and she wraps herself in her blue cashmere shawl.

"Hello, Professor Bart," the padre greets her, wiping his damp face with his cap. She can't decide if he's blushing.

"Hi, Steve," she replies, "those tomatoes look wonderful!"

"Beats store-bought, that's for sure." He holds out an heirloom beauty.

"Store-begged is more like it," Guzmán grumps and takes the sweet Brandywine globes for cooking. "I'll get these inside," he says as he shoulders the crate and retreats up the path to the kitchen.

"We'll pick the basil in the morning," Steve calls after him.

"Tomorrow early, Jesus might come . . . ," Guzmán echoes. "Meet you at the gym in a minute, *al rato*."

Rhoda turns to Steve and murmurs, "I'm sorry for Silvio's ruckus."

"Ah, you heard us," the pastor reaches into the vines to check for stragglers. "Voices carry. Nothing gets by."

She starts as the sea breeze rustles past. *What did he mean?*

Earlier that day as Rhoda excavated the trenches close to the garden, the parson was teaching some new residents how to prune the carrotwood flowers in order to deter the spiked seedpods from maturing in summer. First-time transients often mistake Steve for a gardener. Bosses don't sweat in the sun.

Certainly, some of her university colleagues stumble over how to address him. Plain "Steve," "Reverend," "Vicar"—which is it? His congregation of vagrants isn't a church, not officially. This well-meaning throwback to the New Testament lives a half-hour's commute from the university, traffic permitting. Despite the inconvenience, many fellow academicians need the down-and-out for their research projects. One statistician is attempting to correlate the educational level of residents with the severity of the recession. Laid-off clerks are a bad sign, unemployed engineers and lawyers Armageddon. One pilot study of the newly unemployed includes the recent impact of housing foreclosures.

The government funds the research, especially social agencies that deliver services to clients. Many community programs sponsor outreach efforts and competition for funds is fierce. Rhoda's dig is sponsored by the state because the archeology is of historical value. Expenses for the site museum at the mission are defrayed also—at least the public education component, care of Washington, DC. She's lined up private benefactors as well.

Her ex-husband's the university contact for any charitable contributions, so she stays busy competing for government resources to minimize her contact with Lyle.

Steve comes up empty-handed from the tomato vines and dusts off his shirt. Despite all his time outoors, he's freckled, not tanned. "He's watching us, I bet," he murmurs to her as he unkinks his back.

Rhoda glances around and asks, "Would he do that?"

"He might show up at the gym," the pastor's frown lifts. "The kids are sparring today in the ring. That's where I'm headed now."

She has to think for a moment about who he means. "I worry," she responds, which is true no matter whether it's Juanito or Lyle.

"Juanito will be there," Steve ventures. "He won't miss."

She catches her breath at the name. The two of them head for the ring.

"Don't fret," chuckles the pastor. "We all wear head protection. Come check. And we push school, Professor Bart. No books, no spar!"

Boxing inspired this side of the tracks long before the Settlement built a compact Olympic arena to rally the neighborhood. A contender hailing from nowhere knocks at the door for everyone coming up the hard way, through the ranks. Hope's reborn when an outsider wins. Even churches and police departments used to sponsor amateur clubs.

"Olympic-style boxing isn't the danger," Steve waggles a thumb at the shelter's security fence and what's outside, including Silvio. "Once we set up the ropes, youngsters flocked here," the pastor reminds her, "the tough ones especially! That's where Molca shines."

Rhoda knows that Molca damaged his eyes in the ring, because the kids have videos of his professional brawls. They try to impress him whenever they spar. "How was that move, champ?"

She's noticed how Steve praises his friend, especially when she's around, which reminds her of the loyal Miles Standish standing in as a suitor. She has to smile. Molca's spirit is what's admirable, that's all. He made a name for himself despite the odds, while she was only the second woman tenured in her department. At the college, women's basketball has a better record of hires.

There's a basketball court at the shelter and a league for youngsters—Shelltown loves sports. One of the neighborhood standouts, DeAndra Mayhew, who can rebound and shoot, just won a scholarship to Rhoda's college, which recruits women from across the country. Rhoda coached her for the college entrance exams.

Juanito's sister, Serafina, also attends a university. But Serafina's opted for Berkeley to be on her own.

"I just got a call from my chair," Rhoda thinks out loud. "Talk about another world . . . , light years away. The City Library's only four blocks from here!"

"Kids prefer electronics," Steve waggles his fingers over a make-believe video screen. "Computer games, not books!" But then with a flourish, the priest unfolds a Kevlar cover-jacket from a back pocket. "So try our newest accessory," he brightens. "A nifty stamped keyboard that slips over any book. Ultimate portability"—he grins—"needs no battery. Flip to any page without a mouse. Best of all, print never crashes!"

"What about your literacy campaign to push reading." She laughs. "Invite another guest speaker!"

"Yes, a role model to keep kids in school." He places his hand on her shoulder, forgetting himself. "A celebrity—a professor who digs up old bones!"

"If DeAndra introduces me, I'll do it," Rhoda sighs.

"Ms. Mayhew scored high, thanks to your tutoring!" Steve bows. "A progress report would encourage everyone."

"Okay, I'll put on my school robes," Rhoda agrees, "Play the martyr."

Instead of returning her joke, Steve falls silent.

I meant no offense, she wonders as they walk to the gym. What happened?

The minister wears a collar, which is not how she thinks. He founded the Settlement, though, which she respects. Ancient baskets, pottery, and middens are her church—this collector of antiquities. Solitude is expected. A few faculty and her students are the exception. And Lyle rounded that circle. There's another thought. Before the excavation at the shelter, she never rode the bus anywhere. Even from a car, she wouldn't have noticed the Settlement.

Guzmán, meanwhile, loiters in the kitchen, pretending to clean a window as he spies on Rhoda and the padre in the garden. *What's the preacher's hold on her: doing right by others?*

Molca fingers the curtain like prickly pear but can't let go. He slumps against the wall.

Like a thief and a Peeping Tom, he'll sneak into Rhoda's room again. A junkie sweating over a fix, he'll dry hump his scruples and lose.

"Low-ball sinning," the minister calls such jiving with temptation, empty bargaining.

Outside the kitchen, shadows smear the light, which provides cover for an intruder. *Kids are gloving up at the gym for workouts, which is where she and the pastor are headed.*

On Guzmán's way to her room that doubles as a lab, whenever a resident looms in his path, the shelter's handyman turns to fixing something: a loose door jamb, a light switch, a spill. The residents, though, step out of the way, mind their own business. Apart from Molca's job at the shelter, his go-to repair, he's like a sergeant-at-arms for the residents. No drugs, no alcohol, no trouble! Be nice or the Chihuahua bites off your knees—that joke's on him. Small one, for sure.

Guzmán's in a fog. *The scent of her hairbrush, the touch of her clothes. In an alcove, there's a desk: the computer front and center, a tablet for writing. Juanito gave her an ocarina for a gift, a sweet potato flute. All these worlds are hers. A shaman crossing many doors, her essence remains.*

Molca's hands stay busy but impulse owns him—an automaton robbed of free will, her scent beckons.

Rhoda's not like magazine models—she tucks her hair under a hat when she's digging in the trenches. She doesn't wear makeup. No matter, her features are like the classic statues in Balboa Park carved from marble.

So why does remote control switch on and make him her robot?

You'd never guess that she's a name in her field from the way she plays with the kids. Fact is, for hours a day alone in her lab, she sorts history that no one seems to learn from. He's never met a woman like her—no, not even close. She's a brain and also a lady, yet she won't be run over. Maybe her education inspires that reach. A single fragment of busted pottery can speak for a lost culture—but which one? So she tries on different ways of being a person until the data lines up. There's the nub of who she is, choosing which name to call herself, and when. An archeologist, an Anglo woman, a champion for kids, and there's more—she's patched like a quilt.

Well, *hola, profesora*, here we be, two *mestizos* bridging worlds. I'm of mixed cultures; you're a woman with range. So come on, Athena, put on your Venus. Longing is my science.

Molca jolts awake inside her room. With the key still in his hand, he pulls back her sheets and inhales. Despite the trance from her lotion and perfume, he remakes the bed, while listening for people outside. Her musk lures him to the cabinets and nightstand, although he returns each toiletry item to its exact mark.

In prison, the guards trashed Guzmán's cell during their searches for drugs and alcohol and lewd pictures. All that he owned strewed the bare concrete deck. Including the Bible that the padre gave him. (*The minister teaches Scripture at juvenile hall.*)

Rhoda's presence fills this room. Her baskets and pottery. Her books. Guzmán makes sure that her Manila research folders square up in the old dust lines. A fax machine and copier are always on. Next to the computer is Harrington's biography with Lyle's note. "*I'm trying for promotion and tenure again . . .*" Molca recognizes Carson by sight because "call-me-Lyle" always asks questions that the ex-boxer won't answer. "You want the padre, hermanito?" Molca repeats to the big shot in the suit, wishing that they could go a few rounds.

Across from Rhoda's work space hangs an Indian basket with Harrington's moldy unmailed letters to Carobeth, a stack guarded by a single strand of Rhoda's hair that Molca leaves as a sentinel. The top envelope pleads with Carobeth to halt the divorce and reconcile: that instead of dissolving their marriage, she and Harrington and George Laird continue to live together as they have been. Imagine a dingy apartment for three with the windows nailed shut. While Carobeth and her *nahual*, her shadow double, steal embraces, Harrington looks the other way—there's his answer for adultery. Amazing! How Guzmán seethes.

How can the shell of a marriage outweigh a man's self-respect? Is Harrington's profession worth the shame? Salvaging a few extinct languages and some brittle feathers? Guzmán straightens the unsent envelopes.

Or is his job the reason that Harrington tolerates a sham marriage? A wife proves that he's normal, not a crackpot, since his odd ways are legend at the Bureau of American Ethnology. Convention, maybe, makes him a cuckold—and his salary. After all, in the '20s money was king.

Guzmán pushes one final guess. Does Harrington plead with Carobeth to stay in the marriage because he loves her? Sure, he hasn't shown any affection. Yes, she beds his replacement—one of his research "informants," no less. But consider his stunted meagre life hunched over in the lab. How can a freak say "darling"?

Molca snaps awake beside Rhoda's bicycle, her transportation downtown. He slaps the seat and turns aside. But then, he smells the leather. Women have meant trouble since Guzmán's been old enough to catch a hard-on. A lonely man who does anything for sex chooses badly. He tells himself be smart but lacks discernment. So he's stuck on a wheel that the pastor calls the "lost-cause temptation, low-ball sinning." Even the padre made a bad choice with Regina.

So why does Rhoda praise Steve's better angel, while turning Guzmán into an anthropology project, an informant about the barrio or prisons or gangs? With the padre she smiles, with Molca there's question and answer for her science projects. Guzmán speaks English but not their culture. But he could open their eyes if they gave him a chance. Carobeth wed a genius who couldn't manage both science and ordinary day-to-day life. Does being smart matter unless people connect?

Guzmán imagines a ring announcer barking to a sold-out crowd: Rhoda and the padre are in the front row. *"In the ring he's Molca, the grinding stone; outside the ropes, he's Félix Josué Guzmán, a halfbaked dreamer who likes to read."*

To Rhoda and Steve, despite all their smarts, the boy and him remain a riddle. The two professionals even have a word, "demographics," which means that mixes of people transform a place. Names change, and so do the faces. Good intentions aren't enough to live. Progress doesn't meet half way, or find middle ground. Peace crosses a threshold, tests borders, which involves starting at scratch. You toss out the pilgrims. We'll chip in our own fantasy heritage. Point zero gets us in synch here and now. Where else do we go?

Molca recalls how some women throw themselves at boxers. One named Rita Janowicz wouldn't let Molca shower after a bout—sweat and cuts felt to her like talcum powder. No matter when a match went down, Rita was available.

Sweat and blood are true and real—the only things finally. But they're as much mind as the body.

Rita and the entourage like her is why Guzmán wouldn't take medicine for his high blood pressure after his two marriages blew up. Sure, minus those pills the veins in his eyes might pop and leave him blind. But with such admirers as Rita, no letdown was permitted because of side effects, especially over twelve close rounds.

And so Molca made a choice and blew out his lamp. He lost his peripheral vision in both eyes. The damage only healed part way: He can't see a looping punch coming. Manny wouldn't book any more bouts because of the risk. And then the boxing commission pulled Guzmán's license.

Truth was that Molca blamed his first wife and childhood sweetheart, Lupe Mondragón, for having to quit the ring. Yes, he got beat up when he fought. His style was to wear away opponents like a grindstone, which was why he and Manny kept Lupe away from his bouts. But when he slumped home patched up with staples and stitches and tape, Lupe cried herself to sleep, even after eight straight wins. How could he fight with tears in his head? So he split.

Again, Guzmán smacks Rhoda's bicycle seat. Sure, the professor might have a few wrinkles, but the sap still flows. She's a fighter, or she wouldn't be where she is.

And Molca brings both fists to his chest and takes a standing eight-count. Then, he puts an ear to the door and unbolts the lock. He needs a sharp round or two when the better man wins—no pulling punches. He's off to the gym where he'll throw with the priest!

Although Rhoda and the pastor walk side-by-side past the mission buildings, nothing's been said.

At the Settlement, when the Santa Ana heat breaks like a fever, dusk poisons nostalgia. The good old days cloud over, if they ever were. Worn grudges return, a childhood lost over a summer, too many stretches of drinks or drugs, a string of broken promises—scars never forget.

"Excuse me, Reverend Bentham," Lyle Carson looms outside the gym from the falling shadows. "Do you have a moment?" Both men are tall and lean, equally matched.

Lyle nods at Rhoda merely.

The minister's not surprised: Lyle keeps up with university projects that apply for grants. Charging the investigators rent for their college offices and collecting overhead fees is good as gold. Another cycle of government money has been posted for eligible applicants. Local agencies are primed for the competition.

"The youngsters are sparring, and we need to set up," the padre points to the door. "Come inside, if you box."

"Golfing gloves preferable," Lyle smoothes his tie. "teeing a ball. What about meeting later, say six?"

"The cleaning crews roll out at seven sharp," Bentham counters with an official smile. "Can you call tomorrow?"

"There's some urgency because of the funding deadlines," Carson turns off his loud cellphone. "All I need is a moment," he blocks the door.

Bentham's face flushes. Woodview Theological Seminary ordained him a minister. But Lord help him; this snob needs correction.

After a few moments, though, Steve grins like a choirmaster who can't raise a ruckus when someone's off key. *Suffer the children*, that's from the gospel. "My evening schedule is posted out front," he tells Lyle. "Our cleaning team makes three stops tonight."

"I took the liberty," responds Carson patting a vest pocket. "I'll drop by then."

The minister nods at the arm in his way and waits for Rhoda to go first. But she demurs and stays behind, though the pastor's not happy.

"What was that?" Rhoda asks her former husband after Steve's goes inside.

"Just trying to serve," rejoins Lyle, with a nod.

"Serve what?"

"The future," he insists, flicking away the top of a dandelion. "Lost causes leave bones in the dirt, Lily!"

"Don't call me that," she snaps. "You're not entitled." And his cold expression startles her. Once he used to take her sailing, when their schedules allowed. Outbound together late night—no land in sight, daring deep water with only the stars. Pent up wonder freed them both. Mornings were tender.

And at the gym, for a moment, someone peers back from the past. But then nothing. Lyle's coffee complexion splotches angry red.

"This Settlement has to come down." He circles an arm. "Box seats aren't cheap; neither is parking. Do I have to draw a picture?"

"Ah, Lyle, who decides the meaning? He has a calling; you want promotion."

"So you are soft on this Elmer. He's not your type."

"Honest is my type," Rhoda counters.

"Whose culture of reference, Rho? In China, there are traveling marriages."

"'Forsaking all others' means just what it says, Lyle."

"Speak anthropology, Rho—there are different ways to build a boat."

And Rhoda waits a moment. "Don't hijack science just so you can scratch an itch." She turns to leave to cancel the dialectic. Riling up others is his means of controlling an argument.

Lyle scoops up a blown scrap of newsprint. He grabs her arm and whispers, "Research, Professor—not charity work."

"The university's not for profit." She jerks away. "Not everything's about money." Rhoda can't decide if he's jealous or just acting.

"The college awarded you tenure," he says.

"His master's voice," she replies, cupping an ear as if she heard a whistle calling a dog.

"Things are what they are." He shrugs. "'Resistance is futile.'"

Just then, as the overhead lamps flicker on, Guzmán steams out of the dark with a bad conscience, ready to brawl. While sneaking over from Rhoda's room, he's overheard everything between the two—Lyle especially. How he aches to mix it up. Lyle reminds him of Silvio who hides his nappy hair under a baseball cap. Guzmán shaves his scalp to be done with it. Lyle pays a stylist for a buzz cut and mousse.

"Are you all right, Professor Bart?" Molca asks her. Hot as he to pick a fight, better not get in her way. She takes care of herself.

"Yes." She nods. "I'm done here."

Molca holds open the gym door and keeps his eyes on her, instead of mad-dogging the scholarship boy. Lyle glares at them both.

As the steel hatch narrows and shuts, Guzmán faces down the bigger man who's well dressed, well educated, and well spoken. Everything's perfect. What a waste.

The metal portal slams shut. When he turns around, Rhoda's already up front.

At ring center behind the ropes, the priest demonstrates how a boxer counters a puncher which is today's sparring lesson. He's reviewing Doc Manny's "slide, glide, and tenderize" technique. In order to avoid a head-to-head brawl when anything can go wrong like an uppercut, a head butt, a shot to the kidneys, the smart fighter "slides and glides," ducks to his opponent's flank, and digs hard body shots in combinations. Neutralize power by punishing the ribs. That stops a bum rush.

Guzmán grabs the ropes and mounts the canvas. It strikes him that he's their patsy, their footman, meaning Rhoda and Steve, the two brainiac lambs.

"Okay, Padre, let's stage a two-minute drill!" Molca ducks through the strands and takes charge. "We'll show the troops some moves!" The flyweight dances on his toes to limber up while he pistons both arms. Once he's front and center, he spots Juanito who's sitting at the timer's bench.

"Let the professor glove you up, Padre," Molca points to Rhoda. He waves at the boy who's come out of hiding just to be here with the team. One of the volunteer coaches steps up as Molca's second.

The youngsters hoot and applaud.

Guzmán's and the padre's shirts come off, the recycled twelve-ounce gloves are laced up, and the ties taped securely. The headgear and mouthguards check out.

When Juanito sounds the bell, as the appointed timer, the pair touch gloves mid-ring. Then, Molca pounces and digs some stiff punches into the preacher's ribs. "School's in," he grunts. "Show the kids," he smacks Steve's kidneys.

The preacher's flat-footed in the eighteen foot square.

"Come on!" Guzmán taunts him. The snap of his punches echoes. "Pay attention! Keep up."

Juanito's wide-eyed, and the students stop cheering. Doc Manny's not here to referee!

Molca shifts upstairs and plinks the preacher's chin, which sets him back reeling. The padre's thirty-pound advantage and longer reach aren't good enough.

The preacher's eyes are set. This isn't just practice. As Molca swarms forward, he tries to meet him punch for punch. The gloves snap as they land toe to toe, and neither retreats. Two blows to one is Molca's pace. Wincing from a combination to the diaphram, the pastor throws wild.

"One minute," Juanito warbles, a wing broken. Both are his friends.

Guzmán pummels Steve's chest, clinches, and draws him in. "*Do not pick a fight with the quick tempered,*" he mutters from the Book of Sirach.

The preacher shakes his head and holds on. And then as if from a dream, he responds from memory, "*because bloodshed means nothing to them.*" Then, Steve gathers himself, dances on his toes and shoots the jab. When Molca charges again, the preacher ducks to the flyweight's blind side and pounds his body. But his arms turn to lead—several punches graze Guzmán's flank.

Guzmán returns a stiff combination that wobbles the pastor's knees and mutters, "Why be like you, Mister Miss?"

"Time," Juanito screeches, sounding the bell. The class inhales in unison.

The two fighters remove their mouthpieces and suck in air; then, they touch gloves and bow. Blood trickles from the padre's nose. Guzman's stomach and flanks are dialed with red welts.

"You did good, just like Manny taught," Molca tosses a towel to the padre.

"That was just practice?" Steve pants.

"Feint and throw," replies Molca, wiping his own brow. "Bell rings, you react *a la fregada*. Come on, Padre!" Guzmán cajoles. "Don't *gringos* whack each other loopy, then shake hands. Keep up. Be the good sport!" He parts the ropes for an exit.

"God alone is just," Steve groans as he bends through the strands. "My right hand not so much!"

"Feint and throw, amen," Guzmán follows. "That's true enough, for now."

After they dismount to the floor of the gym, Guzmán musses Juanito's hair. The boy's lashes are wet. And then the ex-flyweight holds out his gloves. The boy cuts the adhesive tape binding the wrists and unties the laces.

The students already have paired up, hoping that Molca doesn't demonstrate on them.

"All right, *chamacos*," Guzmán sings out to the choir. "Turn to your partner and advance throwing punches. Not hard, like a laser. The red corner returns body shots easy and slides and glides just like the padre did. Not hard, *suave*, to fix the technique in your mind. Remember, Olympic boxers use their brains! Clean blows score points."

"Okay, enough," Guzmán orders, after a few minutes. "Now switch places with the blue corner."

Next he tells the class, "Work through four repetitions apiece: each of you repeats four times! Then we spar. The padre will referee. Give him a boxer's applause!"

The kids thump their chests with one gloved hand.

And then Guzmán announces, "I'm off to school."

"Saved by the bell," wisecracks one youngster from the ranks. And the others laugh yet set to work.

"Remember your ABCs," Guzmán sings out. "The mind fights too!"

Molca turns to Juanito, holds out his leather mitts, and asks, "Will you watch *mis rezos*, champ?" Juanito beams and takes the set.

Guzmán whispers the obvious, "Doc Manny's not here. Don't worry, we'll find him." When the boy starts to follow, Molca advises. "Stick with the padre!"

"Doc Manny's got cancer," offers the boy. "He needs us."

"You need to be careful," Molca replies, not mentioning why.

When the boy tries again to follow, Guzmán signals a standing eight-count and taps his chest. He grabs his backpack and strides fast out the door. The next bus is leaving for his social work class.

During all the commotion, however, Juanito slips away.

As Rhoda calls out, Steve wobbles to a chair, still woozy from the ring. "Get Juanito," Steve says, "I'll be okay."

5

OUTSIDE THE GYM, Rhoda searches one direction then the other. Uphill, the shelter residents gather in the dining hall. Sunset bleeds out to the West. Streetside, the flood of traffic has turned, rush hour thins.

Again she calls, "Juanito."

Close by the garden, near the spot for Doc Manny's chair, is where Rhoda first met the boy. One sunrise, when she broke for coffee, there he was. A Spiderman T-shirt rummaged from a bin and frayed shorts—no jacket. Desert nights chill down, even by the coast. She wore a sweater. The archeology dig went round the clock because the shelter was scheduled for demolition unless the courts intervened.

"Hi, I'm Rhoda," she offered. "Are you all right?"

"I'm waiting," the youngster murmured.

"For whom?"

He shrugged and didn't answer.

"Where are your parents?"

He shrugged again.

"I'm an archeologist." She held up a pointing trowel and a household dustpan. And because he was small, she added, "I dig up old bones."

"My sister's going to college," the tyke replied, as if he was the teacher. "I want to go too. That's an ammonite, yes?"

How old are you? she wanted to ask, four feet down in a trench. Despite her credentials, she stood corrected about how much he knew. When she reached down to show him some calcified worm castings, he had disappeared.

Early morning or not, she went straight to the minister who was at the chapel. The boy's name was Juanito Andrés Téllez. His father Silvio had passed out in a bar, probably. Which was why the kid was abandoned. Not for the first time.

"Can't you do something?" she fretted. "He's a child."

"We welcome Juanito here, day or night," answered the padre. "There's a bar down the street. But his father resents us. The boy has family, Professor," the minister answered her frown. "He's not an orphan, not exactly. There's no word."

And back then Rhoda thought, *How sad*. But now that Harrington is her mission, she serves the unsaid too.

When she returns to the gym unable to find the boy, sweat and musk own the place. The pastor's still seated with a towel to his nose. Blood trickles into his beard when he leans forward to stand.

"He's hiding, I bet," Steve says, wiping his lip. "It'll be dark soon."

"Upside down," she replies, "this damn place!" Rhoda presses a fresh towel into his hands and fumes, "This sport is for kids?"

"They need an edge," the pastor replies. "Trouble finds them otherwise."

"Guzmán didn't go easy on you," she blinks hard.

"Molca's intense," the padre answers, buttoning his shirt. "That's who he is."

"Everyone's mad," she muses.

"From Silvio on down," agrees the padre. "Let's go check outside one more time."

The minister stands up again, but it is too soon. If Doc Reese were here, he'd offer a styptic pencil to stanch the blood. It takes a doctor to steady the crew.

Rhoda retrieves an ice pack from a cooler, which he wraps in a towel and holds to one nostril. After a few moments, when he checks the stained fabric, he motions to the volunteer coaches to carry on with the sparring. The less they know the better.

Steve pretends not to notice Rhoda wiping her eyes. "Silvio's daughter Serafina—did I tell you her story?" Rhoda nods yes, but he continues. "Every spring the Settlement honors our students. In front of everyone her father gave her a choice: refuse our cash scholarship or be disowned. She chose college."

"There's someone else gunning for you," Rhoda says.

"The Alliance of Churches and the developers!" Steve tests his bruised jaw. "Quid pro quos for Jesus. Brother James Hannity wants us evicted."

"What about my university?" Rhoda asks, referring to Lyle's ambush at the gym. "Why the hurry?" She doesn't mention that Lyle called Steve "Elmer Gantry," an imposter evangelical on the make.

What did Rhoda and Lyle ever have in common? Steve turns to ask. But he stops. Open that door, and there's Regina, his former wife. Steve failed her, his God, and himself. "I married you," Regina screamed once. "Not this Settlement. I thought we would have a life."

"But this shelter's my calling," he replied. "You're my wife."

"God wants me a pauper? We own nothing except our clothes, thriftstore no less."

Once they filed for divorce, Regina asked, *What if she dated others before the final decree, or did more? Why not nullify temptation by mutual consent? Aren't their vows an act of the will?*

So they tried to treat adultery like a stipulation in a contract.

And the presumption failed. Conscience can't be brokered by attorneys-at-law. God alone is just.

Now the reverend suspects that Rhoda's archeology has dug up old bones—John Peabody Harrington's most likely. Although Rhoda's discreet about her projects, Carobeth's book sits on her desk. And lately, Rhoda's visited Harrington's museum on campus, which can't be by choice for all the bad memories. Plus, the boy goes online to research the archeologist.

Yet the minister says nothing, not simply because he worries that the law has been broken. Losing the Settlement is not his dark night, not this moment. No, what he fears is suspicion that turns on itself, a dim bent that corrodes intimacy. Make your life a beacon to God and beware of presumption. The Good Book calls it sin.

What he realizes is that he's attracted to Rhoda who's intelligent and right-minded. Science is her calling, but she's not marooned in a lab. First and foremost, she's a lovely person. And yet, courage fails to tell her. More than Rhoda's and his differences about faith, their distinct professions and worldviews, a shadow intrudes that is neither guilt precisely, nor shame, nor regret. Silence, perhaps, is better for everyone—words unspoken, things unseen.

6

HIDING IN THE cofferdam built to support Doc Manny's fountain, Juanito brings both fists to his chest, despite his wet eyes. Show the referee that he can continue despite a hard punch. His father can't bring the bulldozers then. Stay scrunched up and quiet in the concrete box, small as a mouse. The worst won't happen. Though Doc Manny's real sick, he'll find his way back to the shelter. Then Molca and the padre will really shake hands.

When Molca and Reverend Steve last sparred at the gym, their fists left red welts. The stripes looked ready to burst the skin. And both of them are my friends.

Blood tastes like tears mixed with earth. Molca calls it red sauce.

My father calls me a girl.

Late nights at home, if my father shows up, he smacks his lips as if his teeth don't fit and talks to himself. He stumbles around to find food in the kitchen. His squawking is a warning. Mother screams, "who is she this time?" We kids know what's coming—the shrieks and the hitting. I try to not be there: to think of happy things.

My big sister Serafina has gone away to college, and I miss her.

Padre Steve lets me hide at the shelter. Though he doesn't know where. When my father shows up yelling "Juanito," he never says, come home, son. He wears the belt. And once I'm home, it's get me a beer. *Apá's* always thirsty.

"My dad's gone to sea, or he'd give me lunch money," I whisper to the other kids at school. "There's wars, don't you know, in the Person Gulch." *(I've seen the soldiers' metal arms and legs right here at the mission shelter. I don't mention that! I can keep secrets.)*

"Besides, I'm not hungry," I tell my classmates, "I had a big breakfast."

During lunch, I ask them for their orange peels, but I only do it on a dare. Right in front of them, I chew the rinds.

When recess comes, I go to my secret place—under the classroom, under the school. I go outside and duck behind the big white oleander bush by the window, then crawl under the wood floor. Outside, there's a hole in the ribbonwood trellis, the trellis that's nailed to the foundation wall. Kids aren't supposed to go there, under the school. The cool bare dirt smells of the dark. Dust shines in the checkerboard light. No voices, no eyes—I float in the quiet.

The bitter taste of the orange peels sticks to my teeth. I am with myself.

Under the classroom, under the floor, after I chomp the orange peels, my stomach cramps. Back in kindergarten, I messed my pants. I didn't dare ask to go to the toilet while the teacher read to us. A grown-up was talking, so I shouldn't be seen. My mind was real loud, but I froze to my chair. If I raised my hand because I had to go, the other kids would laugh.

Under the school, with my orange-peel stomach making me sick, I have to lie down in the dark. Should I throw up—run to the crapper? Call for help? Ask God to forgive my lost prayers? Then I belch. A long long belch. So much air comes out I sound hollow. Yet I'm okay—so much better I feel all right. I crawl outside and go play jump sticks with the other kids.

Here at the shelter, there's a drum in my chest. I wish I knew about Doc Manny. Where he's gone. That he's all right. I'm sure my pal Molca will return from his night class—though he's mad at the padre. Molca's our coach. He keeps us going.

At my apartment in Shelltown, when the electricity or water turns off for back money, Molca pays the bill. Who else would pay cash for us? So I'm sure it's him. Plus, every Christmas and Easter, my mom wins a turkey or ham, with all the fixings, from the supermarket on Estudillo Street, sometimes even a huge rib roast tied with string, hot in the shiny baking pan. How's that for luck? She tells only us kids that she's won a prize, not my father Silvio. Most nights my dad's gone anyway. And he makes fun of the family next door for accepting a Thanksgiving Day bird. "Charity," he snorts. That gobbler's a gift from the shelter doing good for people on *el día de los gracias*. So we kids say nothing about our big feasts on *Noche Buena* and *Pascua*.

To return the favor for the surprise dinners, I bring Molca a sandwich plate with a *pavo* or *carne torta*, *chorizo* dressing, and a *tamal*. We two carry lunch to the garden, and he plucks fresh greens for a salad, quick as I choose which ones. He asks me in Spanish and English for the names.

We wash the *verduras* clean at a faucet, and our hands. Peppery raddishes, sweet carrots, lettuce and spinach and chard, all bright green on the tongue, but each tasting different—we share the meal outdoors with our fingers. His knuckles are bumpy as a rough old tree.

And in the buried cofferdam, the boy taps Molca's boxing gloves, Molca's pair from the ring. They smell like salt seaweed after a storm.

Guzmán lets him try on the leather sometimes, ties the laces, and then presses the left and right mitts together. "That's us, *compañero*," he says. "We're *cuates*, like twins. We're a team. No contender makes it alone. And keep your guard up, no matter what. Protect yourself!"

7

AFTER RHODA AND the parson call off their search for the boy, she walks back to her room checking the shadows. Juanito's father is on a bender now that he's out of jail, falling down drunk. The youngster will hide until it's safe to come out.

Once her door's locked and latched, Rhoda brews coffee. She won't sleep anyway with so much on her mind. A splash of milk, half a teaspoon of sugar—a long stir. She saves the used grounds for her potted fuchsias and wipes down the hotplate. Doing that helps slow down and take a breath.

Rhoda's thoughts turn to Emelia, the boy's mother, as she sips from the hot cup of Kona. Rhoda's met her twice. Once in public, when Silvio bullied his daughter over a scholarship. And the other, when Rhoda found the boy stranded outside a cantina down the street, stormed inside, and took him home.

"Baby him, little lady," Silvio smirked over his beer, mugging for the other patrons at the bar. "Return him to his mother. He belongs with the girls."

The boy let go of Rhoda's hand. After she escorted him outside, he meandered down side streets on the way to Shelltown.

"Where's your father?" Emelia flung open the door when they arrived. Rhoda didn't have to knock. "That *desgraciado*," she muttered, safe enough with a witness. A lamp smoldered behind her. The tired woman murmured thanks but did not invite Rhoda in. Once the door slammed, the porch went dark.

"You kids go to sleep," a voice screamed, twice.

A child's fort made of cardboard boxes crowded the stairs, and Rhoda almost fell. She waited for her vision to catch up.

Back at her room, Rhoda puts down her coffee and shakes out her hair. She gives a laugh-whoop. *Where's my hat?* There's too much sun inside. And this mission shelter is the noisiest place ever, all the ruckus. Front and center is her college, the edu-factory on the mesa, that's running off vagrants to sell a stadium. Lyle's playing ball at the behest of big donors. The Alliance of Churches and James Hannity demand that Steve resign and turn over the keys to the place.

What's worse, the pastor and Molca just bloodied each other at the gym. Steve, though, shrugs it off. Plus, he turns the other cheek with Silvio who's out of jail on probation. *Why not call Child Protective Services? Who suffers then?* she muses, *Who loses? The noisiest place ever, right here. Unscrew this bulb*, she thought as she rubs her forehead.

She laugh-whoops again and sweeps up some loose coffee grounds.

Rhoda's first course in anthropology introduced the notion of a "speech act," including an unvoiced command, a sly call to behave. The idea wasn't easy to grasp. "Helpful articles are on reserve at the library," replied the graduate assistant. "But not mandatory."

The class required that students provide their own examples of "illocutionary prompts."

Rhoda's initial thoughts turned to her mom's house rules. From the time Rhoda turned eight, she learned to be tidy and neat. Her mom raised two daughters by herself, and held down a full-time job at San Pedro Harbor. At ten, Rhoda took responsibility for the laundry and picking up her room. Thelma welcomed initiative—but not with everything. While Thelma left sex education to the schools and romance to novels, restraint and self control were the subtext.

When Rhoda reached menarche, the message was understood: "Don't get pregnant in the bushes and leave me a wreck. Be home by ten. Don't worry, I'll be up."

In her thirties and a tenured full professor, Rhoda introduced her mom to Lyle. She asked him to call her "Thelma," but she called him "Professor." Later, when she and Rhoda spoke through the phone, Thelma wondered, "Lily, he's all about ambition. Is he angling for something?"

In her bed at the Settlement, with the lights off and her eyes closed, Rhoda recalls the beachside restaurant where she told her mother about the wedding. Rhoda wasn't asking for permission. Her mom knew full well who had proposed to whom.

Thelma sipped her iced tea before she spoke up, "I want you to be happy, my love. You're my pride and joy." They talked for a while about the preparations. The ceremony would be a small, for family mostly.

Her mom took her hand and said, "Whatever you decide, daughter. An unhappy marriage is a second job."

"Mom, you married twice," Rhoda replied, not wanting to argue, especially when Thelma felt poorly yet wouldn't see a doctor. "Why fret? I'm all grown up. I love him. We share the same profession. Has that ever happened?"

They were seated at a table by a bright window overlooking the beach. Rhoda poured from the damp pitcher of iced tea.

"You're the one doing the giving, daughter," Thelma patted her arm. "Always it's you picking up the check, not him. Both his parents are lawyers, even if he's only an assistant professor. Probationary, at that."

"Oh, Mom, Thelma," Rhoda responded, "you like Lyle's parents well enough. And what's wrong with ambition? You managed an office when you went back to work."

"We shipped cars," replied her mother. "You're a tenured full professor. His parents are fine," Thelma countered. "The Carsons don't joke about sex on Polynesian sailing canoes or whatever. And when they came by the house, they brought a fine chardonnay and a red, if you recall."

"Everyone likes presents," Rhoda parried the warning about one-sided gifts.

Thelma's jade pendant and matching earrings glowed like the ocean, with the seashore as backdrop. Rhoda topped off their tumblers and envied the waves.

And back at the shelter, in her bed, Rhoda thinks, *I'm seasick from doubt. My life is a thought experiment with a checklist.*

Before her Harrington discovery, she built a quiet life, especially after the divorce. Thelma named her from a novel about the Gilded Age in America when people married for money not love. Love—what's that, really?

Words like *love* confuse people because names take on a life of their own, as if they're things like chairs and knickknacks. Science isn't immune from that fallacy of reification. The term *gravity* conjures up sub-atomic particles called Higgs bosons (imagine tiny invisible hands reaching out for each other). But that picture's incomplete. An Uncertainty Principle rules the very small, while planets orbit a star right on schedule, obeying Newtonian physics. Reconciling those two worlds, those different scales of size, has yet to be done.

Gravity's a paradox, the mystery of attraction at a distance. And simply put, an attraction baffles her too. In Pastor Bentham's view, science doesn't need God and suspends belief to test ideas. And doubt is a flaw, not a method of inquiry.

And yet Rhoda still has dreams, like other romantics. The pastor, by the way, who's not bad looking, also is true to his word. Service to others anchors his faith, not passing judgment. So can lovers speak different languages and be together? Love is as love does, no matter one's country. Plant a garden, regardless of passport—harness opposites.

Rhoda's quest is living true to an "as if" world, where a fact can't be separated from a point of view. She's an anthropologist whose icons are Ruth Benedict, Madame Curie, Lise Meitner, and Rosalind Franklin, all researchers. Although there's Mary Magdalene too. Each of their lives questions power and who stands by the gate. What woman shouldn't read from the margins? The notion of relativity implies more than physics. And the null hypothesis includes Lyle.

As for Steve, he founded this mission because he's "a bed-and-board Christian." He jokes with the newcomers, "This shelter's my cathedral. That's why we paint every spring."

Rhoda has lived alone since she graduated from college. The few men that shared her interests just seemed to float through her life. Even after she and Lyle married, each kept a place of their own. Depending upon their schedules, they shared time at her home or his.

The university has always centered her life, the marketplace of ideas. But both the provost and her department chair expect scholarship to pay. Lyle's in that league now, which is why Rhoda prefers to be by herself.

At a shelter, though, there are voices always. At curfew, the dark's a magnet, so many thoughts. Sometimes she can't sleep. Money's not the problem, nor losing her job. How many women set their own hours? Her independence, nonetheless, comes with a north and a south. At one pole, solitude thrives by itself. At the other, loneliness waits.

Thelma never pushed Rhoda to marry. "Put a ring on your finger and know how to type," was Mom's advice for her girls. A stay-at-home wife was an idea from the '40s. Who can afford it now? Thelma rejoined the workforce in the 1980s when two incomes paid for the Cold War, husband and spouse. After she was widowed, her salary was a lifeline. She sent Rhoda money for college, when she was able.

Thelma's firstborn, Deirdre Alicia, became a nurse practitioner and wed a pharmacist. Thelma displays a hallway of photos. "Here are my grandchildren—that's Alicia and her husband, Tony. Mark is three, and Anais is just a baby. Oh, that's Lily with her diploma."

Deirdre was generous to her little sister with advice about makeup and fashion. She passed along magazines that featured attracting a mate.

Thelma's own mother, Alexis, let it be noted, was a stay-at-home widow who never remarried. Her husband's railroad pension let her keep her home. Both sons fought in Korea and used their veteran's benefits to enroll at the university. Although money was tight after the factories slowed down, grandmother Alexis sent Thelma to business college. Thelma shared such stories while she ironed and sewed, welcoming her morning shift at San Pedro harbor off-loading cargo ships.

Rhoda's grandfather, Paul Raskin Bart Sr., had been a merchant seaman who ferried lendlease supplies to Arkhangelsk and Murmansk during World War II. His ship was torpedoed off Russia. Rhoda's great-grandmother, Alice Rasmussen, tagged cargo in Oakland for nine years. She married an island man named Emekona Kamanu and moved to Kaua'i, where they built up a small fleet of refrigeration boats. Although they had no children of their own, they raised a boy and a girl born to Emekona's two sisters. The native Hawaiian practice was called *hanai*, and the children considered them their parents.

Rhoda's interest in anthropology was homespun because her family spread out all over the globe. And once a cousin or distant relative lived overseas (the Philippines or Australia, for example), they were never the same. They went native. Thelma's visitors intrigued Rhoda—and made her feel strange. Odd habits were legend in foreign countries. Sampling fertilized duck eggs, *balut*, however, or tasting witchetty grubs stretch boundaries. These odd odors and tastes challenge convention. Accept a new normal and there's no set point. The eye changes.

Rhoda's biological dad, Paul R. Bart Jr., sailed aboard container vessels, yet Thelma claimed that absence steadied their marriage. For all his coming and going, they managed to buy a house. And although Thelma cautioned her daughter against sailors, Thelma's second husband, Andrew "Andy" Michaels, served in the merchant marine. One voyage lasted six months and eight days. Rhoda remembers her mother never looking better than when the men were at sea.

"A sailor's wife sets a table for one," Thelma offered when her younger daughter left for college. With Rhoda setting off on her own, Thelma sat in the dining room staring into her wine glass. After her second husband's funeral, Thelma had shuttered the kitchen.

Taking meals alone doesn't bother Rhoda; it's no small triumph.

To obtain her doctorate in anthropology, Rhoda persevered for eight years. And once she found a teaching position that offered tenure, she fought for five more. Thelma quit encouraging grandchildren.

At Rhoda's and Lyle's wedding, which was held outdoors at Torrey Pines, the bridegroom made a joke. "What's the difference between matrimony and a monument?" He paused and surveyed the guests. "One lasts for all time; the other does time."

Thelma flinched as if shot.

Who were you mocking Lyle? Rhoda wonders, *yourself? I recognize finally what should have been obvious. Joining Phi Beta Kappa doesn't make us humane.*

"An unhappy marriage wears like a second job." That sentiment's care of Thelma who taught her girls, "get that ring but learn how to type." *Infidelity,* the word is grounds for divorce; betrayal, the fact, is a kick to the stomach.

With Lyle in the picture again and Rhoda battling insomnia, Thelma advises therapy. Her mom sighs, "Thank heavens you're strong, Lily. I did one thing right." Regarding a psychologist they disagree: Rhoda no longer trusts experts. She begins with one question, Who cleans your house? How can you trust anyone who doesn't do the laundry, Einstein included?

About eight months ago, Thelma ignored her family's concern about her chronic abdominal pain. Doc Manny visited the house and recommended a woman internist, Dr. Fagan, whom Thelma consulted. Thelma's reserve and no-nonsense style, perhaps, is why she wrote to Rhoda after the tests. "My dear, the good news is that I fit into all my old clothes. The bad is the cancer!"

And Rhoda clutched her mother's letter because what leapt to mind among a welter of feelings was writing an article about death and dying. Today, her mom weighs ninety-eight pounds and coughs into the phone. Nonetheless, Thelma still insists that Rhoda's career comes first, especially now that she's on her own.

"Career?" Rhoda murmurs, as ghosts wander through. Do our parents have to die before we start making a home?

8

FAITH CAN BE a moral hazard—isn't that an odd thought, especially coming from a minister who just took a shellacking in front of the team? A stiff jab tempers pride. The righteous confuse conviction with faith.

And he recalls Regina, long before they were married, cradling her warm cup to her cheek while listening to a God-strucked boy. That's him at twenty, when the two of them staffed the front desk at the Old Cottage Inn, a landmark hotel. They were co-workers who had just met on the evening shift. How must he have sounded to her?

"Imagine Jacob's Ladder in our backyards—a staircase for the angels. God's message is hope. But we can't wait on miracles."

"We all have a purpose," was Regina's pet phrase. She hummed songs from musicals like *South Pacific*: "if you don't have a dream . . ."

He told her about his plan to enroll at Woodview Theological Seminary in Salisbury and bring God's kingdom to earth as Jesus did. "Make day-to-day life a beacon of faith. Stand like a Knight of the Ordinary!"

There was her silent liquid gaze as if life was elsewhere. Had she heard him?

"This is the New South," he explained. "Consider North Carolina and our progress with including everyone. Let me attend a seminary like Woodview that broke down barriers."

She glanced around as if someone might hear.

Late in their marriage, when they slept apart in other rooms, he would wonder if injustice mattered to her. She wanted people to be happy and loved things to be neat. Yet she neither cooked nor cleaned nor helped with the garden, and the grimy streets downtown depressed her, although she enjoyed the back alley laments of T.S. Eliot and Leonard Cohen. Was she open-minded and tolerant of those on the margins, or easily tired by extremes. Neither pursuing a career nor going back to school motivated her, which was true when they married. She preferred to stay in her room and read. At the

Settlement, however, supplicants appear day and night in all manner of need, so Stephen kept the manse tidy, on top of the other duties that kept him up late. Yet no matter the hour, Regina always waited in bed. So he set up a cot in the rectory.

When she complained about his long hours at the mission, he asked, "Why comfort the comfortable? I choose the gospel and an active ministry."

"You founded the Settlement," she answered. "It's been six years. Served beyond all endurance. Can't we move on?"

"The poor aren't a phase, Regina. They're a calling!"

"So I'm bound in a shoebox?" she replied.

What do some residents mutter at the chapel? "Too much Jesus." They're right. He chose her vocation.

Steve tests his sore jaw as he prepares to lead the cleaning crew that tidies and buffs highrises. *Molca beat you like a drum*, he eyes his reflection. *At least the boxing team learned something. Blow your nose, champ.*

And the minister muses about vanity and appearance. He's the foreman for a night shift of jobless residents. No one cares about his looks. Wiping the bathroom mirror costs a stitch in his side. Worse than pride is Moon-Calf idolatry, exalting a graven image of faith instead of sanctifying ordinary life. Wearing a cross and not putting others before oneself.

And the thought sits him down.

Stephen Robert Bentham married Regina Filipa Hardesty and took her for his helpmate and wife. Starting a family would serve a higher purpose. He and Regina would stand arm in arm in the footsteps of Abraham and Sarah or Mary Magdalene and the Nazarene. Make day-to-day life a beacon to God.

That vow had inspired his ordination as a minister. Thus, a simple transfer to an established parish, assuming the good work of others, was not enough. Striking out on his own was a means to found his own congregation, his own flock.

Unlike the apostle Paul who lamented that it is better to marry than burn, Stephen welcomed a partner. Joined in matrimony, sharing a mutual goal, husband and wife exemplify *koinonia*, loving compassion. Everyday life buries people, robs them of purpose. His distrust of routine could be sanctified, made dutiful.

But he's ahead of himself, as usual.

When he and Regina first met as staff at the Old Cottage Inn, Regina was living at home. She had no plans for the future and was comfortable with her parents. As for Stephen, his family's printing business could afford a small paycheck that met his expenses. Saving for the seminary required a second job.

Each evening after they clocked in; the front lobby had to be picked up, as well as the adjacent American Chestnut Room with its cavernous stacked fieldstone fireplace. Regina cleared the random cup and glass from the antique tavern tables burnished by generations of use. The gray lustrous wood required special care. As she wiped and buffed the grain, nothing else registered; she was so rapt. Touch owned her and little else.

He tried not to stare. Her expression made him guilty.

What was she dreaming about? he wonders years afterward, *Gone with the Wind and the mansions?* Many changes loomed in their lives—for him, above all, the ministry. Their university town was growing fast. Even the heritage antebellum hotel had joined the computer age. Amid all the clamor, the Bible was a life vest, and the *Word* is safe haven.

Stephen and students like him considered themselves part of the post-segregation modern South, forward-thinkers whose reaction to the Civil War centered on the future, not past battles won or lost. A century and more beyond Gettysburg and the famous address honoring the war dead, what did it mean to form "a more perfect union"? Such a charge tosses a brass ring at the moon because it begs another challenge. How to make a nation better one person at a time? That crusade was to scale! To perfect your country, perfect your neighborhood.

Steve's take on his birthplace Chapel Hill is personal. His father, Landon Bentham, owned a small printing shop, which had been his father Augustus's before him, and his father Luke's before him. The women in the family were famous, or infamous depending, for championing suffrage. That struggle for the vote fueled more than a few family arguments about equal rights and a number of legends about the Bentham women.

Great-aunt Esther, also his mother's name, was picketing a polling place when a cloudburst struck. A county clerk named Lester Ansel, who was also a Baptist deacon, peeked out at her damask parasol and intoned, "Go on home, Miss Esther, get out of the rain."

She stepped to the porch and stood her ground, "Come out of the dark, Mr. Ansel. Stand with us; join the future!"

Now Steve's father Landon wasn't a traditional head of the household. He groomed his daughters and his sons for college, if they were willing to work. Teaching his wife how to set letter type and print on paper vexed some of his workers. Esther already excelled as a scribe of oral history, especially weavers and dressmakers, midwives and herbal healers, and the "mourning ladies" who prepared the deceased for their last viewing.

Some of his fiercest critics were men of the cloth. Landon opined that conscience doesn't line up in pews and never joined a congregation. That cost him customers. Nonetheless, church-going was optional for his family. He did collect sermons, though. The house, in fact, was crammed with books, tracts, and newspapers. Steve's mother, Esther, collected women authors from select magazines. One of the family's proudest accomplishments was printing small literary journals and pamplets that championed equal rights.

Coincidentally, one of Stephen's required college classes referred to the Scottsboro trials in Alabama in the 1930s. The reading list included a scholarly article about a local magazine from that period that had demanded justice for the defendants. Stephen emailed the scholar as part of his course research, a history PhD in California named Professor Philemon, who mailed a copy of the magazine's masthead, which Stephen's father recognized right off. In turn, Stephen forwarded some old galley pages from the family's print shop. Professor Philemon, an American Studies expert, was researching a book about how small presses and magazines helped fuel the Civil Rights Movement. Their correspondence was one reason that Stephen stopped in San Diego and visited Lemon Grove where the Mexican American community resisted segregation in the 1930s.

Regina, his promised bride by the time of his sojourn, loved the pictures of America's Finest City: Spanish-themed Balboa Park and the Prado, site of the 1916 World's Fair, the Panama-San Diego Exposition, a panorama of the North Island Naval Airbase taken from the windy bluffs of Point Loma while a marine amphibious hovercraft skimmed the channel. He included a sweeping vista of the seacoast from the Mount Soledad cross that included moored research vessels that had returned from all over the globe.

Since Regina and him were engaged to be married, she mentioned a honeymoon there.

Stephen didn't describe the early mornings downtown when maritime fog shrouded the streets, and the homeless materialized out of the murk, mud people morphing out of the walls of a cave. So many camped on the sidewalks that he tightroped the curb. But by the time the early haze cleared out, so had the wraiths, although they flooded back again with the setting sun.

Vagrants cramp tourists, Professor Philemon, the history professor, noted when Stephen asked about the daily exodus. Vacationers come to dream in the sun. Theme parks have no Apocalypse World, at least not yet. An unofficial truce in the city saved appearances: out by sunrise, in by nightfall.

What leapt to mind was Luke's gospel. *"Whoever has two coats must share, and whoever has food likewise."*

Professor Philemon smiled like her lips were salty and said, "Come to California. Try your luck. We're famous for a fantasy heritage."

The term *fantasy heritage* haunted him during the separation and divorce from Regina, who was a good woman but not the wife he expected.

Hypocrite! he condemned himself, *Moon-Calf Idolator.* Concoct a wife to serve your calling, then sleep alone in the rectory. Serve the slipshod good. Put the welfare of strangers before your own spouse.

But no matter how he flayed himself, he could not salvage tenderness.

Finally, when he told her that he wanted a separation, she looked up with red-rimmed eyes and said, "I'll curse you 'til my dying day."

Stephen fell into a depression and couldn't eat or sleep. Regina moved out to an ocean-view apartment near Tourmaline Park, or rather Guzmán and Manny Reese rented a moving van and took care of all the details. They urged him to take some time off. Instead, Stephen threw himself into his work, and tried not to dwell on the past. Yet even after several months, he hadn't taken down her picture. One sunrise, Guzmán found the priest kneeling in the garden with his head in his hands. "Get a grip, man," the ex-boxer snapped, "Gather yourself! A hundred people need food and a bed."

"I broke my marriage!"

Molca hunkered down in the dirt. "Yes, you did. Not because of adultery nor wife beating. Besides, do motives matter? Your wife's not the person you imagined. And neither were you."

"How can I atone?"

"What's done is done," rejoined Guzmán. "You both suffered. And like the lawyers say, you pay her expenses. Compare the folk here at the Settlement!" Molca rubbed some earth into his hands and thought for a moment. "She has her consolation."

"Maybe there's hope if we talk?" Stephen said.

"You cut her loose; there's no going back."

Steve looked over at Molca. "But I can't help thinking."

"Damn it, man, don't make me a pimp. Regina's dating, get it? Not divorced that long, and she's busy catching up." Molca avoided the word for a pent-up woman.

Stephen slumped in the furrow. "I pushed her away; it's my fault!"

"Jesus," Guzmán groaned; "Quit sticking the camel with needles! This shelter is for people with no place to go. For twelve years it's stood—you're the steward. That's the call."

And Molca broke off a switch of seeding basil and slapped Stephen first on one shoulder then the other. "I dub thee a Knight of the Ordinary! Step to the list and champion these folk. Join up with Doc Manny and rally the small!

"Live true to your name, Sir Bentham," Molca winked. "The prospects are good!"

And then, as Guzmán walked the minister to the kitchen to help prepare the evening meal, he shared his divorce from Lupe Mondrágon, his childhood sweetheart. (The Settlement's physician had been Molca's best man.)

Molca's sense of loss has always struck the minister. As young as he is with no family or friends, estranged, absent belief or trust in a higher power. Perhaps his multiple cultural legacies invite doubt about which side is right or wrong, true or correct. Molca claims that the story from *Genesis* about Eden is about acceptance, not religion. The apple is a down payment for a sense of belonging.

Such jibes inflame people. Guzmán's nickname Molca is a fighting word in itself? Is it a boxer's nickname or about being Chicano or a hand implement to make guacamole? Ambiguity pisses people off because they assume the joke's on them. Guzmán's mixed inheritance is obvious, the fact that he speaks English and Spanish. The name Molca is in your face.

And yet consider his short career. No proof's required about being here today and gone tomorrow.

Since Molca's style was to trade punch for punch, he took a pounding in the ring. Each and every bout, after he was patched with catgut stitches and metal staples and surgical tape, his young wife Lupe wept. And because Molca couldn't fight with tears in his head, she stayed home. After a bout, he slept at the gym until he looked like himself, which took a while, depending.

After one brawl for big money in Phoenix, when Molca returned to their apartment, Lupe had cleared out. He searched all through Shelltown, but word was that she had left for Texas. Somewhere like Dallas or Fort Worth maybe, staying with a sister.

Half a year later or so, when Lupe's attorney served him with divorce papers, Inéz Santos had already moved in. Why so quick? Manny Reese, Guzmán's coach and mentor, had warned Guzmán to let the cuts heal.

Did Guzmán love Lupe and miss her, or couldn't he live alone? Who else but Lupe understood why he had stabbed both his parents with that ballpoint pen—his mother Florencia screaming at her husband when he staggered home late; his father Eduardo drunk with lies.

(The pen is mightier than the sword he once told Lupe, when she asked if he was sorry for the assault. The joke made her cringe)

Molca's father never should have married; his mother never should have stayed. A whipping marriage doesn't let go—the fear and regret. And maybe finally, that's why Lupe left him and cleared out—scared for Molca or of him and dreading the worst, probably more besides.

"Quit smothering me," Guzmán's second wife, Inéz, protested while Guzmán was recuperating from the televised set to in Tijuana with Ernie Davis, a bout that bruised his kidneys so bad that his blood pressure shot up past the red line again. Doc Manny put Molca on diuretic pills to reduce the swelling in his feet and hands. And until no blood showed in his urine, Manny wouldn't let him train or run.

Marooned at home, Molca was a pain in the ass—he realized that. Watching videos, reading ring magazines, and surfing the Internet only held his attention so long. To make up for his foul moods, he had been buying Inéz flowers every week. A clean orderly house was her doing, which was why the washer and dryer were almost brand-new. Guzmán had even bought a forty-inch ultra-slim television on credit so that she could watch her Spanish *telenovelas*. Marrying a woman meant taking care of her. But presents go stale, even under warranty.

"Give me a baby, Molca," Inéz pleaded in bed.

"When I'm a contender, maybe," he rolled away before the finish. "Not now."

"I hate when you do that," she hissed.

"You won't take the pill or let me use rubbers. So what's left?"

"I'm a good Catholic," she retorted. "And you were baptized too!"

"My kids pray with their fists," Guzmán blurted. "Hand-to-hand, that's how people live; God's will isn't good enough!"

"If you had talked like that before, I would have run!" she answered.

Despite their impasse about children, Inéz did get pregnant. Pissed as he was when she turned up late, Molca assumed that he had been a few seconds too slow. But in her sleep for two nights, Inéz called him by another man's name.

Molca hired a detective with a camera who shadowed her for days.

After Molca received the pictures, rather than put his fist through a wall, he bagged his equipment and left. Three-time losers go to prison if they reoffend. There was his time in Youth Authority, a DUI when his cousin was blown up in Iraq, and now Inéz's birthday surprise.

He fled to the gym, which was locked up, squeezed through an air duct on the roof. The heavy bag rocked from his punches like a tall palm in a brisk Santa Ana wind.

Why can't a heart take hard shots like his busted hands?

Hours later he snuck outside and walked for the rest of the night. So what if someone robbed him. Gun or knife be damned, He didn't care. Let them try! Near dawn, he stumbled upon a fleabag hotel near the Coronado Bay bridge. A musty mattress on iron springs; one folding chair and a bent card table; a black and white with only three channels. The refrigerator barely kept a six-pack chilled. No matter. After Inéz betrayed him, he spent so much time at the gym and trained so hard that he always made weight. Manny's attorney advised him that under the law he was the father of the child, no exemption. But he could file for a divorce and petition the court for a DNA test.

After a month and a half at the fleabag hotel, Manny insisted on setting him up in a nice condominium and retrieving his things from the old apartment, although Molca assured him that he could move stuff himself. His next fight at the Olympic Auditorium would put them in the big money. So why screw up with Inéz over his few belongings? All this shit had to mean something.

He and Inéz did meet with a marriage counselor, but Guzmán heard the whine in his own voice when he asked Inéz who was the father. That tone brought back the teasing when he was a boy. Scrawny and quiet, he didn't make friends. The Mexican kids called him "*mayate*" because of his deep complexion and kinky hair. And yet the blacks nicknamed him "Ollie" for coffee with cream. The Asians said nothing and stuck with their own.

"Stop crying," his father sneered when the same bully bloodied his nose every week after school. "Grow some balls, and get even."

"Does little baby want some *teta?*" his mother joined in and tugged at her blouse.

And the padre recalls wondering, *Why tell me this story Molca after I wrecked my marriage with Regina? Are your hard times meant to get me through? Go ahead and turn the tables on a pastor: Offer a parable about drowning and rising from the dead!*

Right now before the night shift cleaning highrises, as Steve tallies the struggle to keep the shelter open, the notion of a boxer sharing a parable strikes the minister as proof of the Holy Spirit, the thought of a layperson preaching to a preacher. Jesus might have taken heart.

Outside the rectory, a horn blats from the street summoning the cleaning crew to assemble for work. The skyscrapers are waiting. The parson bows his head and clasps his hands for a moment before he runs for the van, and on the way he throws a right then a left. He'll need the Almighty before this shift is over, and more besides. Wolves are out, and the devil too.

9

THE BUS DRIVER scowls in the rearview mirror. Although Guzmán just yanked the exit cord for the stop on Palm Avenue, he waves the driver on. For a second, during the ride back from night college, Molca thought he saw Manny Reese, although the glaring fluorescence flooding the aisles screens the dark streets. False alarm though. The man in the hat is too young. Molca grabs a seat and wipes the window glass, still searching.

If you look at Doc Manny straight on, you'd guess that he's in real estate or horse racing, definitely not a boxing promotor and coach—his lined face is tanned from the outdoors, and he's a fine dresser. Sharp suit, crisp shirt and tie, and always a fedora or Panama or tweed, even a pork pie or straw weave, never a stetson. A bit worn or not, all his closet is quality. His style is classy yet quiet—he makes an impression without standing out. No one guesses that he's in his late seventies. Ask people what he looks like, and they describe his clothes, which is how Manny prefers it.

Molca's bus crawls past a derelict warehouse boarded shut from the tuna cannery days and slashed by graffiti.

Manny's out there hiding somewhere, probably out of his head from the bone cancer that robs him of red blood cells so the blood turns pink. The pain gets so bad that he swallows handfuls of prescription pills. The synthetic opium, however, scrambles his brain. Then, he's convinced that the CIA and the Office of Naval Intelligence plan to spirit him out of the country, lock him away.

What scares Manny the most, though, is not spy wars. Instead it's the Milgram Experiment from the 1960s that demonstrates the frailty of the conscience. Hire volunteers to work in a lab where they supposedly punish students who make mistakes. The researchers convince the volunteers to administer electric shocks to the learners that are in another room. The experts urge the volunteers to raise the voltage, although pleas can be heard. "I have a heart condition!" "Obey authority," the volunteers are told, "Turn up the dial even if the cries stop." The volunteers don't know that the entire test is a ruse, the so-called students included. Manny's conclusion is bleak. Empathy is more than human, less powerful than the weak force in atomic physics.

Lieutenant Commander Manfred Saul Reese, MD, USN, retired, has his own story about following orders. He never came home after his military service, not the way he was forced to retire. One of the demands was a signed pledge to observe the National Secrets Act or face prosecution. During Manny's cancer treatments, however, he wanders in time, which is a side effect of the drugs. Both the preacher and Molca serve as his caregivers.

Manny's treated sailors with rare tumors and ruined immune systems who were stationed aboard warships monitoring ground zero tests from miles away. Even through goggles, they saw the billowing radiation Xray the bones in their hands. And during secret experimental trials in island jungles, aerosol germs blew the wrong way and contaminated hunters. There's a nerve gas designed to incapacitate terrorists that causes epilepsy if anyone breathes a few parts in a million.

Manny's generation ushered in factory science during the 1940s. Compare that achievement to ten thousand years ago, when bands of hunters sharpened flint weapons by hand. Consider how the Greek philosopher Archimedes lay seige to Greek fortresses with catapults and battering rams. In the eighteenth and nineteenth centuries, pioneering experimenters studied electricity and the propagation of light as curiosities. The modern twenty-first-century laboratory patents its discoveries like a business, and the military adapts weapons from cutting-edge research.

When Manny resigned from the navy, he retained copies of his patients' medical files as insurance. Who would accept that modern weapons have fatal aftereffects, not just for the soldiers? Long after Manny left the service, he never carries a cellphone so that he can't be tracked. Consider the danger. He knows firsthand about midnight renditions and black prisons.

Guzmán first met Doc Reese, alias Manny the Hat, at sixteen when Guzmán was locked down in Youth Authority for assaulting his parents. In custody for five months while serving a sentence, a probation officer escorted Guzmán to a holding area where Manny introduced himself as a boxing coach and manager. Guzmán recognized Manny from watching the boxing tournaments inside the walls, a welcome break from a cell. All the guards addressed him as "Doctor Reese." The boxers called him Doc Manny.

"I hear you can fight," Manny cut through the prelims, all business.

"I can do that," Guzmán eyed the well-dressed *anciano* who carried himself like an athlete, despite his years. And Guzmán added, "In juvenile hall, you make room for yourself. Asking please doesn't cut it."

"Care to try out for the boxing team?" Manny said. "Reverend Steve put in a good word. No use, though, if a fighter won't take orders."

"Can't punch if you don't train," Guzmán countered. "Me and the padre, we mix it up in his Bible class! The man's been to seminary and must be thirty. The King James he gave me is back in my cell. If God's in this world show him to me! Light up these dingy walls."

The hat man half smiled as if he'd heard already. He tapped the paint and confirmed, "You got his attention."

So where has the Doc gone missing these last few days? Guzmán falters, as he watches people from the city bus. Has the military confiscated those medical records? Soldiers who question do disappear.

Molca's ride inches past a strip mall that's vacant mostly, except for a liquor store and a payday loan joint. From the window seat, Guzmán peers inside at the customers.

Although Guzmán's forehead is pressed to the cool glass, his eyelids sag, and his mind wanders. He's imagining the Hollywood Breakfast-at-Tiffany's music that Manny plays in the gym when the kids train. "Quit grumbling, my huckleberry friends; punch the bag," their coach challenges them during the workouts. "Sing with your knuckles! Rap out a tune."

Guzmán wipes away the window steam and rubs his brow with the water. Trouble with night class is the snap between worlds. Just a while back, in the Reserve Reading Room doing homework on post-traumatic-stress, he felt himself dozing off. There on the library table was a novel. Some French guy in Algeria shoots an Arab at the beach.

John Peabody Harrington leapt to mind, the man obsessed with holding back death, his own and the extinct Indians. Molca read more of the novel and kidded himself, you and that guy Meursault are salvage. Who's coming to the rescue?

The novel's pages were dog-eared, probably for a quiz, which seemed funny in a sad way because an Arab flashes a knife at Meursault from ten feet away, and the Frenchman shoots once, pauses, then pulls the trigger four more times. The aimless light forces his hand. Nothing matters.

So okay, Mr. Golden Gloves, Guzmán zings himself aboard the musty rapid-transit coach, *What's important to you? Doc's disappeared and doesn't* want to be found. Plus, the preacher's left you high and dry while he's sparking Rhoda.

Sure, Manny and Steve helped Molca win an early release from jail, and they set up some paying fights that made a decent living. Molca's grateful for the push. But after every bout, Manny collected his 15 percent commission. As for the padre, figure this: Who's the go-to guy at the shelter? Here's a hint: he's ethnic!

The French novel gives Molca pause—a citizen executes a native.

Yes, fool, Molca mutters to himself, *"You're the Arab!" Check out the other passengers on this number eleven route.*

And then, as Guzmán tries to rest in his seat, he conks out. At least that's what he assumes after he jerks awake by the window of the coach. *Here we be, Manny, we wrecks and do-gooders—flung together. Thrown-ness, that's a term from some German rector, or was it Ezra Pound?* Ride public transit gentlemen, and test yourselves about underdogs!

The bus driver's scowling in the rearview mirror, but this time he's on the emergency radio, probably talking to 911 or Homeland Security. Molca wipes drool from his chin and assumes that he talked in his sleep. Several passengers shrink back in their rows like he just pointed a gun.

Certainly, Guzmán's not asking the two skinheads with Nazi tattoos seated in the back row. Nor the headband and bandanna, red as blood, hunched by the exit door. Maybe they're night students too, but Guzmán's the one toting books.

At this moment, they're all stuck in Palm Avenue traffic, so Guzmán guesses that he's only zonked for a minute, a catnap, no more. *Doesn't matter, though,* he thinks, *pull that E-cord and bail!*

Once Guzmán dismounts to the curb, darkness pulls the plug, so he waits for his night vision. Across the way, beyond a canyon, looms a rainbow haze of city lights. One corner's dark. Construction on the stadium's shut down in that block, at least for now, because of a gasoline leak underground. The adjoining street is closed, but the sodium lamps are still lit. That's where the boxing team jogs for stamina. Under the vague reddish glow, bicycles are free of cars, kids team up for soccer or play street ball.

At least there's open space, until the spilt gasoline's cleaned up and construction resumes.

A police helicopter rips past on patrol. Panic grabs Molca, plasters him to a spinning tilt-a-whirl like at Belmont Amusement Park

His head races as he hies for Broadway Street downtown, hustles back to the shelter. The cops are on the lookout, he bets. Just then looms a bar, *Club Eso Es*, smelling of sweet and fiery *mole* sauce, hot roasted peanuts, and fresh-popped *palomillas*. The place seems familiar, Guzmán ducks inside.

Five figures slouch at the counter drinking beer, while two couples sit at tables in the back.

Guzmán nods at the barkeep, orders a cola, and sits down by the front. A cork in rough water just bobbed ashore. Sea noise from the freeway washes inside. All of the city is inside a shell.

The bartender glances over a few times as if they've met before. Or is Molca paranoid? *Are those punches adding up, Mr. Golden Gloves?* Meanwhile, a couple in the back orders another pitcher of margaritas and crisp *chicharones* just out of the fryer.

Molca's stomach growls, but he has to wait. At this joint one buck and seventy-five cents buys some sizzling pork rinds salted and dusted with chili. That's U.S. money. Molca fingers his loose change and chews some ice. Maybe the padre saved him a plate?

"Hey, *joto*," erupts a voice beside him, "This is a bar, pussy. Supermarkets sell sodas."

Guzmán grins, holds up his soft drink and says, "I'm on the wagon—doctor's orders."

The drunk knocks away the glass, which soaks the table.

Guzmán dabs at his shirt and stares at the mess. The drunk's grinning inches away—*Molca* smells pork rinds on his breath. *What leaps to mind is a kid hoisted up on a bartop by Silvio who taunts him about whether he's a boy or a girl in front of the other drunk borrachos. Only when the kid pulls down his zipper to expose himself and protest that he's a man does the session end, with laughter.*

The bartender flies round the counter calling out to two patrons, "Tito, Cuevas, *ayuda, por favor*. Come on, Gerardo, let the man be. Nobody gets hurt."

"I won't hurt this *puto*," barks Gerardo.

"Bet on it," returns the barkeep, offering Guzmán a hand towel and wiping up the wet table.

Molca's on his feet ready to unload, that's how close he comes to decking the clown. Bell rings, you react. But this is a bar. Cold cock a civilian, and go to jail.

The two jumpy patrons lead away the drunk. "Show our boy Molca's picture by the cash register," the barkeep tells them, "the ring poster."

"I thought I recognized you," the bartender offers Guzmán a chair and wipes sweat from his own upper lip. "Sorry about this *fracaso*," he repeats as Guzmán fidgets from the rush of adrenalin. "Your manager likes our tamales, so he donated that souvenir on the wall, autographed too. Where is Manny the Hat? We used to make book on which top he'd be wearing. Does he still volunteer at the health clinic on Crosby?"

"He likes to look sharp," replies Molca, who just got a lead on his missing friend. A few drops of cola tip from the glass.

"Refill?" the barkeep offers. "On the house. And we got *pozole* soup fresh-made."

"*Gracias*, no," returns Guzmán, "maybe another time." He's headed for the health clinic this minute, no matter if it's closed. As he leaves, voices follow him outside.

"Your little man ain't shit."

"You ready for a hospital, *panzon*. He'll put your big gut in traction."

Standing on the curb, Molca checks the scene. Passenger jets stretch out in a landing pattern to the southeast; their lights lined up to the horizon. The barrio health clinic is in the opposite direction, a half-mile down a few cross streets. Strange that Molca forgot that free clinic, which is where Manny treated the padre after methamphetamine pills hooked him.

The clinic staff stuck out their necks to help with the padre's detox. So Manny, who had just been discharged from the cancer ward himself, insisted no questions, no leaks, no nothing. Any inquiries about the pastor, refer them to me. Silvio's a nosy informer itching to make trouble.

As for the pastor's addiction to "speed," Molca blamed himself for not noticing the obvious. Steve's ex-wife was dating again, enemies wanted the shelter property, and the reverend barely could get out of bed; he was so down.

Someone must have offered, "Take these pills, Padre. You'll be your old self!"

And then suddenly, Steve's working round the clock day after day, skinny as a rail, teeth going bad from the methamphetamine. Unfortunately, Doc Reese was not able to intervene since a blood clot in his lung sent him to the hospital. And by the time Doc was back on his feet, the minister was strung out on crank.

Sending a parson to a detox program for meth addicts was not an option. Imagine if that story leaked to the media. Television cameras, reporters, sharks smelling blood. The city would confiscate the property. The Alliance of Churches would assume supervision of the shelter. The minister's cure had to be hush-hush, and the barrio clinic was tucked away in an enclave of Mexicans and Chicanos. A storage annex behind the facility served as a recovery room: Manny and Guzmán snuck in a cot and medical equipment.

As for the patient, the pastor kicked cold turkey against Doc's advice: the Aztec Cure, which went hard on captives. After this junkie flushed away his pills and went into withdrawal, one person grabbed his arms and the other, his legs, like *Mexica* priests harvesting hearts. Steve flopped like a fish out of water.

"Why haul wood to Golgotha?" Guzmán railed as he held down his friend.

"Don't blaspheme," the priest grit his teeth. And then he joked, "This sinner made his bed."

"Pastor Bentham, we have medication," cautioned the doctor, who looked bad himself from the cancer. "Redemption is your calling, health is mine."

The padre shook his head. "No more chemicals!"

"What do you call a Christian meth freak?" Molca chimed up, as he brought over a chair for Doc Manny. "A hyper-chrit for Jesus!" he told the crew, jittering in place like a storm-tossed leaf.

The priest's laugh retched on hair from the dog as he wiped away snot with toilet paper. Speed freaks are never cured—the craving's in remission only, if they stay clean. Any shelter proves the gospel. Nah, Reverend Steve's detox at the clinic smacked him back to earth. Jacob's Ladder mocked his reach as the stairway to heaven rolled up on a dime.

Once the priest could sit up and stomach some soup, though, his concern was for the doctor who was recuperating from his latest bout of chemotherapy. Which one looked worse? Pale and short of breath, the old doctor's Alpaca suit hung on him. His matching Merino tie fit like a scarf around a pole. Only his gaze retained strength. Once upon a time, Dr. Manfred Saul Reese had healed patients like Merlin cured King Arthur. Battling myeloproliferative cancer, though, drained his magic—he was the one who needed a wizard.

At the secret detox station that Doc Manny had set up for the minister, Molca and the pastor exchanged glances. Then the parson offered the physician a deal. "The Settlement could add a few beds, Dr. Reese, if we had you living on premises."

Manny grinned—Saint Steve's barely back from the dead himself! And he's trying to rescue an old guy from the Military Industrial Complex!

Guzmán and the padre, however, were doing more than a good deed on the sly. Doc has no family, no kin that they knew of. Moreover, where could he find a job, all things considered? His savings were shot. The mission did need a physician on site for medical emergencies. More important, though, Doc needed to convalesce, not just from cancer, but from challenging the Defense Department. In a military town, calling out the Pentagon is risky, better cover your six. The local press is a cabal; knives are out for apostates.

"We're going ahead with building your gym, Dr. Reese!" the pastor chimed up at the barrio clinic. "It's your baby, remember, especially the ring. We need to get it finished."

"You could share my room and keep an eye out!" Guzmán lobbied.

Without doubt, a neighborhood boxing program would be a fine memorial, though nobody wanted Doc to give up. City inspectors, moreover, already had approved the project, assuming that it was pie-in-the-sky. Where was the money? Even a boxing ring costs thousands, which was a laugh. The shelter was on the skids, regardless of its decade downtown.

"We're being run out!" the minister rallied. "Let's turn the tables. You'd get the job done, Commander!" Manny already had donated boxing gloves and head gear. There was the gift of the fountain too.

And the stable of professional fighters that Manny had managed welcomed a chance to help. Several had invested their winnings and owned businesses because of him. One was a sports reporter, and another was a bookie in Las Vegas with a following. Gifts of sports equipment such as heavy bags and weights, help with insurance and construction work—Manny had a list.

"Government grants are in the works, Dr. Reese," exhorted the minister, "and we can raise private funds." Doc knew that Padre Esteban led by example. The pastor had wrangled the blueprints for Manny's gym *pro bono* from a respected firm, a design that was solid yet let in the sun.

"And don't worry about snipers," the minister tested the wind. "You'll be safe in the gym."

"With you aboard, we could lay the cornerstone by spring!" Molca added. "We'll reserve your chair by the garden."

"The birds of spring neither reap nor sow," sighed Manny. "I can listen for hours."

The minister grinned from his sickbed in the barrio clinic liking Manny's take on Scripture. "A little rest for clipped wings," he chimed up.

"I'll rust if I stop working," Doc answered. And he sighed as if he were a patient. "A man's got to keep moving. Or else they find him out." Doc felt trapped, on the outs. Not the least because he had never married, and there were rumors that he liked men. Even Molca had judged him for that. The flyweight hadn't considered himself part of the inquisition, until that moment. After all, how can someone scarred by torches set fire to someone else?

Knee-jerk thinking hurts people, Molca reminds himself. He wishes he had told that to Doc. He hopes there's still time. Wetbacks calling names, isn't that a laugh? Downtown is where he's been searching for Doc, not close to home. Manny wears a hat, and that's okay. A life is about quality not the brand.

"The birds of spring," Guzmán murmurs a few steps from Chicano Park, which is under a freeway that runs north and south.

Every year at the mission shelter mid-city, Doc and the boy hang up old yarn and frayed string for migrating flocks. Right there downtown, they strew the bright stuff from trees and bushes for building nests. Those bits of color keep track of the egg-laying guests. And when chicks arrive, the two watchers hang dispensers stocked with seeds and grain. Even hummingbirds sip handmade nectar from feeders, as well as the honey from the garden flowers. That's Juanito's idea.

Doc Manny calls the spring our "Maestro of Solace!"

Enough of that! The clinic won't wait, Molca thought.

10

AS MOLCA REACHES the Shelltown infirmary, the doors locked and barred; he's mulling over how dreams give out. He can't help it, not with people missing. This place is where the padre spent a hard convalescence a while ago—he chafes his arms. He and Doc told the folk that Steve was visiting Los Angeles on a fund-raiser. "Los Angeles?" Rhoda replied from her desk, but that was all. She was busy wrangling permits for her dig from a slew of government agencies.

Night sounds rise up at the neighborhood clinic: traffic noise, passing jets, a few diehard crickets chirping of love.

That's enough, enough of her, Molca raises both fists to his chest. *Never get stuck on hearts and triangles!* His antidote this moment is to search for his coach.

A high brick wall runs around the dispensary, topped with security lights. But a *sapote* tree in the back overhangs the barrier, with branches strong enough to climb.

Once Molca drops onto the clinic grounds, he heads for the same storage room from the reverend's stay, the one with all the *karma* from the pastor's hard fall. And as Guzmán creeps forward, light filters over the transom, which is scary because of bad spirits.

If you meet a ghost, don't run—ask the message. That's an old Mexican saying.

Right, homes, he tells himself, *why you shaking?*

But then, as Molca holds steady, no one appears; nothing storms out of the light. So is that an old phonograph record or a person singing, 'Til then, please wait?"

Guzmán chins himself up on the door frame and peers inside.

After Molca drops back down to the floor, he calls Rhoda, no one else—and not just because the professor owns a car. Pulling Reverend Steve away from a cleaning crew late at night will get back to Silvio who's working for somebody. For the shelter's sake, doing anything suspicious is anathema, especially with the demolition on hold.

The term *anathema* the pastor would appreciate. The Alliance of Churches has the pitchforks out.

All Guzmán tells Rhoda in code is that a "situation" came up: Can she bring her wheels?

Rhoda quavers through the static, "Is Steve hurt?"

Molca grits his teeth. She's driven sick people to the clinic before, no questions asked. "Talk later," he hurries. He glares at the satellite phone.

Her drive over takes only a few minutes. First thing Molca notices is Juanito sleeping in the backseat. And he smiles, almost. "No bad comes without some good," pint-sized included. The boy came out of hiding after he ran from the gym, must have knocked at her door. Not for the first time. *Querer es poder.* "Home is where the heart is."

Oye pendejo, crotch pube, Molca lambastes himself, *You're stuck on proverbs? Turning sentimental, champ?*

Rhoda dismounts from her car, and Juanito barely raises his head from the backseat. "Wait here," Molca whispers to him, locking the car doors while the boy falls back asleep. She checks the alarm, and he leads the way inside. "Is he okay?" she shivers in her overcoat.

"It's Manny," Guzmán says. "It's the cancer. Two of us can settle him down. He talks to you, Professor Bart."

"Doc Manny," Guzmán whispers once they reach the clinic annex, "This is Molca. I brought a friend. You and her talk science together."

"Hello, Dr. Reese, this is Rhoda. Will you let us in?"

A nightgown peeks from under her overcoat, and her slim legs show.

The door cracks open finally. Manny's linen suit is streaked with dirt and dust, rumpled from sleeping on the floor, and his perfect felt brim crushed where he's bedded down singing to himself. "They're after me," Doc whispers, clutching his briefcase. "They know what I am. They'll toss me in an unmarked grave, throw me over the side."

"It's okay, Doc," Molca says, taking the satchel. "The place is closed. No one's left. Come with us."

Once they lead Doc to the car, he rallies after he recognizes the sleeping boy. When the four arrive at the Settlement, they're on the alert. As they hurry to Rhoda's lab, quiet's the escort.

Rhoda carries Juanito to her couch while Guzmán leads Manny to her bed. As she fetches a blanket for the boy, Molca turns down the covers for Doc who won't stretch out until his briefcase is next to the pillow. Rhoda can't help glancing at her desk and Harrington's basket of secret letters.

Doc Reese writhes under the blankets—the synthetic pain pills scare up bad dreams. "Don't tell," he murmurs out of his head. "Not anyone. That's how they find you."

He's hurting from the cancer, Guzmán figures. He hurries away to scrounge some illicit opium that will relieve the ache in the old man's bones, so he can rest. The streets are the pharmacy when there's no insurance. Molca injected himself a few times without permission.

Juanito doesn't wake from the sofa—Rhoda's thankful. She tucks in the covers light as she can. The boy flinches when people get close.

After forever, it seems, Molca returns, prepares a syringe after dissolving the white powder that he just purchased, and jokes, "Time for a nap, Doc."

"Wait," Rhoda whispers as Molca bears down with the needle, "Why not prescription medicine?"

"No!" Manny starts and tries to leave.

"It's okay, Doc, all copasetic. I'm you intern." Molca hangs Manny's coat on the bed frame. He rolls up the old man's sleeve, applies a tourniquet and swabs down a vein. "Nature here, not big pharma," he soothes, injecting the potion slow while monitoring Doc's breathing. A sterile bandaid follows. And then he turns to the professor. "The government requires names and addresses. That's the way they locate people, and he knows that. He's an expert witness in federal court, remember."

"I have a favor," murmurs the old man, who recognizes his protégé and reaches for the briefcase.

"Don't worry, Doc," Guzmán pats his shoulder. "We're a team." Doc has shared his last wishes and written a will. "We'll put up a headstone ourselves," Molca reassures him. "No military sponsor, period. We won't forget. The professor's our backup."

"In my briefcase, Guzmán, find the envelope. Remember, you and the boy," and Doc falters for a moment as the poppy takes hold. An expert witness won't rectify the past, not in closed court. Justice in secret is the husk of dignity, honor postponed.

Lieutenant Commander Reese counts himself among those to blame for bad faith. In the military, he put on a mask to pass muster, which meant a double life. Doc's Naval career was magic from a hat once he accepted his commission as a lieutenant. A core part of himself was sequestered. He was born before World War II, and his generation ushered in the nuclear age. Then the struggle for civil rights gripped the nation. A sexual revolution followed, but not everyone was equal. Some remained stigmatized, and Doc seethed. Enlisted personnel choose an MOS, a military occupational specialty. Manny was an officer, a physician, and a shadow.

On long deployments across the globe, *sea pussy* refers to sexual relief from any quarter when wives aren't around. Ashore though, such ardor is interdicted, punishable by court martial. The armed forces abide by the Uniform Code of Military Justice; such are the rules.

Existing on the margins inflames the conscience. What's acceptable winks at what's permitted; convention and hypocrisy dance. The military tolerates alcoholics because what soldier doesn't need a drink sometimes? One old salt told him, "I never drink before noon. And I go off base. I'm back aboard ship by reveille."

You're not hearing yourself sailor, Doc thought to himself. *You're defending a drunk.* And Doc wondered, *Who are you, Dr. Reese? Honor doesn't surrender to fear.*

Manny struggled with who to trust and where he belonged. If his secret were found out, his career was over. Shame, perhaps, was why he chose boxing in high school. He recognized his sexual preference, and a fighter protects himself always. Going toe to toe with raw power isn't smart. He read about how the writer Oscar Wilde chose to flaunt who he was and was sent to prison. Manny's alternative was to jab and circle. *Keep your hands up. Open the ring bit by bit*, he thought.

Dr. Reese found out about the secret weapons tests over many years. All the while he was living underground. Patients reported symptoms including skin lesions, losing patches of hair and nausea. He mulled their accounts, crosschecked the medical causes, weighed the repercussions of speaking out. He didn't launch a crusade.

One chief petty officer who reported that he was losing his vision and balance mentioned an atomic test at sea. Towering tsunamis swamped an anchored decommissioned fleet, including battleships and aircraft carriers that were capsized by the flood. A swath of ocean boiled into steam. Miles away, a curtain of spray and saltwater droplets choked his destroyer escort. Thick fog lingered at noon, long after the blast.

Dr. Reese learned of other cases.

At a different naval station, an electrician's mate who suffered from cataracts recalled dead birds clotting the ground after radar tests were conducted from microwave dishes thirty feet wide. Diesel generators bristled with static electricity and shorted out.

Then there was an ensign with a chronic cough and nosebleeds, just out of the Naval Academy, who recalled a remote valley sprayed by air with anthrax bacteria. Feral pigs and goats, stray cattte and horses, all died. The mission helicopters were washed down with seawater, which poured over the flight deck.

Doc logged and reported these episodes and symptoms because of his oath: Do no harm. At the same time, he was a naval officer pledged to serve his country. What is my duty? Who are my people?

Decades after he was drummed out of the service, when he was asked to testify as an expert witness in a class action suit that had been brought to trial, he agreed. Getting revenge for the secret tests wasn't the reason, not exactly. He had left the service and built a career as a bonafide promoter with a gym in the Gaslamp District. And then the padre built the Settlement up the hill. The first time Doc toured the place, he thought of a hospital ship hulled on a reef. *You're retired, Doc*, he told himself. *No, you don't*.

Barely awake from the opium in Rhoda's room at the mission, Doc holds out a hand for spare change.

Defense Department movie footage boils up in his thoughts. Trees doubling over from a shock wave, then snapping back into splinters. Buildings implode and career into rubble. Then the lens goes dark. Is our best hope clarity?

Out of the blue, Doc urges Molca and Rhoda, "Do right by me!"

"Sure, Doc," Guzmán replies. The old man lies back in bed with his help, while Rhoda tucks in Juanito, worrying how much the boy understands.

Manny falls asleep, finally. Molca stashes the briefcase under the bed. He gestures at the two sleeping figures and asks her, "Can you hold down the fort?"

He cracks open the door without a goodbye. His eyes burn. *Can't let his feelings show*, he thought. The padre's buffing skyscrapers with a cleaning crew, sweating word about Doc. The minister likes the parable about the least of us going first—better go remind him.

11

RHODA LEANS OVER Dr. Reese and edges the blanket away from his face. The pulse in his neck shows through the skin. Juanito's asleep too for right now, although Molca just left. She wants to close her eyes, but coffee has to do instead.

From under the bed, she retrieves the doctor's briefcase. There's the envelope with his final instructions. Also, here's a folder with former patients' physical exams that date from his stint in the navy. His official memoranda are attached requesting follow-up treatment and care. There is no reply.

Warriors don't leave the wounded behind. Nor their dead.

On tiptoes, Rhoda puts back the satchel. She recalls that just months ago, Doc led the charge to overrule the city and county planning commission. The board rushed to demolish a row of businesses, two small hotels and the Settlement, by declaring eminent domain. A committee vote was scheduled in municipal hall, despite the fact that no notice had been posted.

Rumors percolated through the social media about land grabs. Virtual space was abuzz about *Big Brother*.

Dr. Reese rallied the opposition, although he wasn't well. Obliged to stay off his feet, he rode a golf cart to lobby neighbors for several blocks around. The appeal was simple: You're next. Your property turns into parking at less than market value. Sports brings in thousands of fans. That's progress. We, downtown residents, pay the overhead.

The hearing room overflowed. Closed circuit television played in the halls. Near the front entrance, street mimes turned themselves into furniture. The silent bidding played to the conscience.

A riot squad was on alert. Police already had set up traffic barriers.

After the meeting was called to order, several comissioners asked to be heard. Only the chair's microphone worked.

"Let us speak; let us speak!" yelled a man in a scuffed leather jacket, clutching a backpack.

Another petitioner in a buttoned suit approached the podium and held out his card.

The head of the commission shattered his gavel. He ruled that the committee proceed straight to a vote to declare eminent domain.

Several audience members, wearing cigar-shop T-shirts with emblems, held up spittoons. "Not on us, not on us," they chanted. "No evictions! No taking land!"

A row of shopkeepers and coffee barristas waved skull-and-crossbone flags.

The police did not intervene.

Doc Manny stood in a corner, calm as an impressario. The coalition had jelled!

One of the commissioners, Noémi Saavedra, borrowed a bullhorn and asked the crowd, "Sports fans, can you afford a ticket? What about you, Doc Manny?"

A couple in gorilla costumes held up a banner: "Self-dealing is no Valentine."

The chair yelled for order.

"Not on us," the spittoons chorused doing the "wave."

Ms. Saavedra made a motion: Pending further study, demolition for the stadium would cease. There was a second.

A tuba honked and growled in the back, played by a Vietnam vet in full-dress uniform.

Three of the commissioners' hands went up when the vote was called. A single abstention stayed the demolition. *Manny had invited each of the commissioners to the Settlement. Share a meal, meet the residents.*

The room exploded; pandemonium carried. The tuba played the national anthem.

Television newscasts featured the fracas. **Anarchy Downtown** headlined the local paper, which identified the "ringleaders" as a radical Latina muralist and Dr. Reese, a medical consultant and professional whistleblower.

Two weeks later, Noémi Saavedra was indicted for an illegal visit to Cuba. Then Manny's apartment was ransacked with no sign of forced entry. A police officer joked, "A shipmate broke in, Commander, high on Agent Orange?" Manny's testmony in federal court about the Vietnam defoliant chemical was supposed to be sealed. The case itself was closed to the public.

"We know what you are and where to find you, Commander." Someone left that message at three in the morning. Just before dawn, a trash bin caught fire in back of his apartment. Manny vacated the premises, with Steve and Molca's help.

For a while, he kept lockers at several gyms stocked with changes of clothes. No one has his address. Doc's stored his belonging at the mission. The boy shares nothing private.

Rhoda checks again on the old man and Juanito, glances outside to make sure they're alone.

Over the course of their friendship, Rhoda's tested Doc's confidence because she's needed advice. When she says nothing sometimes, the silence means something. He reads behind the page, unthinks the obvious, like a scientist questioning a premise. She's told him that the Settlement was once a hotel and that people abandon stuff. He returned a joke, "Archeologists dig up secrets. Doctors bury them."

Her mother trusts him because they're of an era. As Thelma says, "For us, the odd ones kept to ourselves, and then we left Red Cloud for the big city where no one knew us. A fresh start's hard in a village." Neither Thelma nor Manny carry a mobile phone.

This moment, the city seems a wilderness of lights, choked with modern signs. In the Chauvet Caves in Europe wall paintings of prehistoric bison and horses date back thirty thousand years, yet the artistry remains unsurpassed. How many generations is that? Professor Bart's coined a term "archogenics" that refers to ways of thinking that don't change, as if perception is etched in the marrow. Representations of the world are ancient habits of mind. Downtown there's always a nervous edge, danger lines. Traffic whisks along the bordering freeways, and no one dares cross.

Yesterday, it was yesterday, wasn't it? Rhoda had rushed her mom to the emergency room when Thelma couldn't hold anything down.

What began with battery of tests led to the worst outcome. After Thelma was admitted to the emergency room and intravenous fluids administered for dehydration, her condition stabilized. Blood was drawn for a complete panel of tests. X rays and an ultrasound test were performed at her bedside. She was transferred upstairs to the cancer ward on the tenth floor for observation.

That was when her oncologist entered her room, and after a few moments, recommended hospice care for the end of life. Her mom was the strong one and patted Rhoda's hand. "I've known this was coming, my dear. Farewells takes practice."

Rhoda tried not to weep. Why upset her mom? And she thought to herself, A scientist *should know better.*

"Are you okay, Mom?" Rhoda hugged her after the doctor left. *I'm supposed to be rational, able to control my feelings. Ideas go extinct; that's death too. I accept evolution.*

"I can see all the way downtown," her mother said from her gurney near the window.

"I work right there, somewhere," Rhoda pointed in the shelter's direction.

"I'm proud of you, daughter. Doing a kindness for other people. Smart isn't always hands on."

"Making a home is how you taught me, Mom. Dress for company, alone or not. Pick up after yourself, no matter where. If need be, take off your shoes at the door. And bring a gift always, no matter the occasion. We scientists ought to practice how to be in the world. We're all homemakers."

"Anything's possible," Thelma smiled, despite the shock of all hope gone. "Try raising two daughters."

Somewhere in the city the hour chimes. Rhoda's impulse is to call home, but it's past midnight, and Thelma should rest. This moment, the boy's asleep on Rhoda's couch tucked under the covers. His eyelids flutter from dreams.

Where is Stephen? Rhoda wonders as she searches the nearby skyscrapers. Buffing floors is an act of faith, which she understands. Ideals begin with a bucket and mop, On that they agree.

12

"ALL RIGHT, FOLK, next break in an hour," Padre Steve rallies the night cleaning crew, holding up his squeegee and sponge. "Let's rise and shine," he plays with words, pointing outside to the darkness.

"Maybe Becky can keep up this time," teases Narciso, who sold computers before the Great Recession. Becky, a paralegal, used to do research for real estate lawyers at a now defunct partnership.

"Some days being a woman is hard," Becky banters matter-of-factly about lagging behind.

"You're too old, woman, for that excuse!" Reza tells her.

"Wanna check with me on the next pit stop?"

"Take that," Fred guffaws, as they pick up their cleansers and gear.

Tonight in this city, twenty-six stories up, everyone's back to essentials, no matter who they were: Fred, Narciso, Becky, and Reza. Nine sixty-five per hour comes with a flop and a meal at the mission, which beats the bare sidewalks going away.

But gratitude is too simple with a cot for a bed.

Consider Fred. His curriculum vitae these days, his résumé, is a mop and broom despite an associate's degree in electronics and six years experience installing heat and air. Sales went flat, and he was let go. The bank foreclosed on his condo and changed the locks, despite the fact that his payments were current. An attorney couldn't help. His car was repossessed, so he couldn't camp out. With no place to sleep, culverts, dumpsters, or homeless shelters was all she wrote.

"We're sorry, full up" was all he's heard for weeks.

Try camping instead by the river or dig spider holes into canyons for a night's rest.

Fred and three others, with hard luck to match, hot-racked a motel room in El Cajon next to a fire station. During the day, while one team searched for work, the other warmed the sheets. Then at sundown, the evening crew rolled out. On Sundays, switch.

The motel gave four people a push on the sly. For an eight-by-ten room, plus a toilet and shower, two paid although four bedded down. Turn in by shifts, first the blue team and then the gold squad, and keep the place clean. The manager, a former submariner on old diesel boats, understood rough weather.

Then Fred's unemployment ran out.

Twenty-six floors up, to Fred's left, Padre Steve has assigned himself to buffing windows and halls, a task that sets the pace for the eight-person crew and keeps an eye out for mischief. Half of them are new, and not everyone's honest. A cadre of recycled dependables, however, including Fred, Narciso, Becky, and Reza, lead the shift. The padre's not sure how to feel.

Outside this tall building, the night boils with commotion: electric rivers of headlamps and muffled, neon-bright highrises. The thick panes of glass hem the noise. The few blocks marching to the harbor, the few crammed with parking lots, fill and empty in cycles. This tide, perhaps, is why the padre recalls the walkway at the Ocean Beach pier across the bay.

Above a stretch of dark ocean beaten to froth, the pier footpath closed by high surf, a young believer begs for a sign. The thundering surges, the spray of cold salt—where is his life and his mission? Show me a path! Ignoring the crashing waves, he walks along the shaky parapet, distraught by the silence.

Dark billows slam against the footing, the air hisses with fog—and then his soul is transfixed beyond words. Yet he understands: "As you welcome the least, so am I received." The Word was never as clear: The city's streets hide shadow people. And the young Stephen breathed, "Here is Your servant." And thus the homeless tapped him to build a shelter.

First, he took a job at a halfway house for drug addicts that needed a chaplain. Nothing in his experience had prepared him for so many lost people, such broken lives. And whenever frail sobriety and the misery of dependence tested his resolve, he went back to the pier for strength.

That lone epiphany above a vexed ocean endures until this present day, waiting for another sign. For the pastor, though, decades afterward, silence is where mystery resides. Faith, nonetheless, shows the way through the quiet—the Settlement his pledge, to endure. And, Lord willing, grace under fire works its own miracle.

Steve rinses the cleaning sponge in soapy water and wipes the window ledge in short even strokes. Quiet is welcome. When the elevator pings, he glances over and sighs. So much for the prince of peace.

"Good evening, Brother Steve," booms James Hannity, representing the Alliance of Churches, an outspoken lobby of evangelicals with mainstream connections. Hannity's heels bruise the tiles as he strides front and center.

"Hello, James," the padre greets him. "Excuse me for not getting up. It's past midnight. Have you returned again so soon? It's just been a week. But if I sign over the Settlement, you'll just tear it down for a sports park."

"What steward would give the food out of his mouth, Brother Steve, but not think to cook for two?" Hannity smoothes his tie and checks behind him. "Why serve a hundred downtown when you can budget twice that number away from here?"

"We're downtown, and nobody else wants us," Steve takes a deep breath and wipes away streaks. "'Not in my backyard,' say the neighbors!"

"Just a moment," Hannity interrupts and steps away to answer his cellphone.

The volume is loud enough that Stephen hears someone ask, "What's his answer?"

"I'll call back," Hannity replies and snaps shut the set.

"We serve hot coffee from a thermos," Steve unclenches his jaw and stands up, checking his work. "Of course, it's late for caffeine."

Hannity shakes his head, straightens his cuffs, and tries a different tack. "A sponge such as that offered Jesus wine on the cross," he points down at the bucket.

"A sponge dipped in sour wine, vinegar, Brother James. Which was no comfort." The padre scrubs the baseboard with both arms. "Is *Matthew 5* our text again? My moral fitness sets a bad example, so I should step aside?"

"Do the gospels speak to you?" Hannity asks throwing back his shoulders.

"Not like you're speaking now," Steve wipes the far side of the window frame. "My star is the resurrection! The Alliance has wanted me out for a year, especially the latest shove. Your interviews on television, right?"

Hannity turns to look. "All that bad press!" he lowers his voice. "That cost us. We all suffer when our donors pull back. That's why new leadership is best for everyone."

"The corporate Jesus and the board of apostles," Steve drawls. "'Righteousness sells: Look at our numbers!' But I won't resign. I bid you good night."

"Reverend Bentham," Hannity bares his teeth in a smile, "Don't be a fool, Lord willing! You're outgunned. We are many; you are just one. The Settlement is welcome to taxpayers' funds. The rules say that eligible social agencies can compete for grant money. And new RFPs were just posted. But the proposals are due right away. And character witnesses can spoil an application!"

"The Church of the Holy Gotcha," Steve wrings out brown water. "Gossip and rumors serving the Lord. Your cathedral has a lock on forgiveness."

"The decision to move is yours, Brother Steve, win or lose. But a few clever ads with the kids can't save the Settlement this time." Hannity's referring to the shelter's advertising campaign that turned back "God's firm," a nickname for the Alliance.

Also, Juanito's zombie video went viral on the internet which brought in donations and public support.

James Mathias Hannity loosens his collar and steps up for the kill. "Jesus was a *tecton*. You know that term from the Greeks, reverend, a handyman, not just a carpenter." Hannity points at the washbucket. "But old houses wear out repairs and have to come down! Betcha' Jesus could pitch that job.

"Now, sports are for the common good—which is why the Settlement built a community gym. But progress is larger than coddling a few delinquents. So join with the stadium or get out the way. Don't condemn the obvious when the obvious sells!"

Steve paddles the water and waits.

"A clever public relations campaign won't protect your people, reverend. What are the shelter's expenses? How long can a mission stay open without new grants-in-aid? What if the courts rule in our favor about eminent domain?"

"You're the one in a hurry, not the Settlement," Steve replies. "We plant our own vegetables."

"Do us all a favor, Pastor Bentham," Hannity clasps his hands. "Come to your senses. Other cities are lobbying hard for government funds. Yes, time matters. Join with us, sign over the shelter, and we'll appoint you to our board—on full salary." And Hannity raises his eyebrows and smiles.

"Let me work, please," snaps the padre.

Hannity tests the window ledge with his fingers, grins, and dusts them off. "Stay in grace, reverend. You have our card." He pats Steve's shirt pocket. "And do watch your temper!"

No one in the crew says a word as the floor buffers whine and wastebaskets clatter. Busy or not, though, they heard Hannity's threat to close the shelter, and someone has a mobile phone. A text message is posted on the shelter's web page: Don't count on a bed. Look elsewhere. BOLO 4 place 2 sleep.

The padre tries to get back to work, although he's listening for the elevator doors to signal Hannity's departure. Only then does he dry his hands and check for streaks.

The pastor scans the bay from the skyscraper's height. What about these hundred souls? Where will they go? A few months past, the Alliance might have forced them out, if it hadn't been for friends and some luck. But Doc's gone missing, and Hannity's stirring the pot. This watchtower's almost done. Dawn is hours away.

"What time is it?" Manny Reese starts from a deep sleep after his rescue at the barrio clinic and sits up in Rhoda's bed. She's dozing in her recliner chair.

"The kids are being photographed at six this morning!" he tugs at the bed covers. His eyes are wild again, several hours after Guzmán's street-medicine lulled his panic. "Some reporter came by from the television news. I forgot which channel."

"I'm right here, Dr. Reese," Rhoda whispers, pointing to the sleeping boy. She retrieves an accordion folder from her desk, next to the computer. Manny understands documents—that's how he thinks.

"That television coverage is long past," she murmurs and extracts an old Sunday edition from one file, a trophy from months ago. Back then, the newspaper also covered the boxing team doing their roadwork, the jogs along the city streets for building stamina. Those photographs and others at the gym helped turn around public opinion about Steve's divorce. If the kids believed so strongly in him, the pastor had to be doing something right.

She turns on the bedside lamp and offers Manny a glass of water.

"Someone called out, didn't they?" he asks. "Woke me up." He sips a few times and hands back the rest.

And Rhoda wonders what do military physicians dream?

"I worry about Steve," she admits.

"Ah, the padre. They're out to get him too.

"Here's a photo of the kids jogging at six-thirty early," the doctor points to the newspaper photos, squinting at the date on the page. "That stretch of road passes the stadium. For now, the construction's on hold."

WORDS UNSPOKEN, THINGS UNSEEN

Juanito shifts on the couch, and they wait for a moment.

"That's Molca leading the pack," Doc Manny resumes. "The padre and I provide escort in the van. We steer clear of cameras," he glances at the boy. "Juanito's the one who dreams up videos. He and the kids."

And while Doc Manny checks the photos, he makes sure that his briefcase is close.

Rhoda hands over a copy of an old letter-to-the editor complaining of street walkers and addicts that mingle downtown.

"The boxing squad looked sharp." Rhoda puts on her glasses to read. "Hit the books, or no spar!'" she quotes from their interviews. That slogan is Manny's about putting school first. Grades decide who works out or not.

"Champions, these youngsters." Manny nods. "Our zombies came to the rescue." He winces as he props himself up and smoothes the fuzz on his scalp.

"We need another miracle," Manny whispers.

What happened was this. Being kids, the boxing team played hide-and-seek at the park, in the poison oak bushes where they shouldn't. They blew up like balloons, because they scratched the itch. Their faces especially. Scarlet welts wept like wounds. Juanito's eyes were almost swollen shut; the other kids dripped rheum.

Being youngsters, they asked for pictures before Doc Manny treated the allergy. Their ruined faces, especially. As Rhoda obliged with her cell, they lay down outside the clinic and scraped their backs on the rough concrete.

"Only zombies sleep on sidewalks," Juanito called out to the team. "Zombies, not people." Comic books were his inspiration. And this cry supplied the voice-over for the Internet video.

Juanito uploaded the content on the web after he added spray posters as highlights to its slogan, "Save Our Shelter!"

And as luck has it, well-wishers' checks, large and small, helped pay down the gym. Even a piggy bank arrived from a six-year-old, a trophy that's displayed in the front office. Donations continue, especially around Halloween, addressed to *The Sidewalk Zombies/The Young Dead.*

Rhoda checks on the boy again. He didn't ask for permission to go online, He just posted the videos. He learned computer modeling from Rhoda and her students. She taught him how to map an archeology site in three dimensions, a bird's eye view of a dig.

"Surprises keep coming," she muses out loud, "city elections are soon."

"Politicians follow money," Manny sits up and dangles his feet from the bed. "And their districts don't want us. They prefer that we stay where we are and not move.

"Excuse me, Professor. I need the bathroom. I'm in my skivvies."

"Let's get you up and about, Dr. Reese—I need your help." She offers an Afghan blanket. "I feel guilty about asking."

"There's the magic word, 'guilt,' so I must be okay?" He searches her face.

"I have to be honest." She opens the box. "There's a secret."

"Which one?" He nods. Patients can't hide much.

"I discovered a cache of Harrington's research right here at the Settlement."

"Ah, Harrington," Doc Manny confirms, "the linguist who cobbled the dead."

"The man of a million pages," agrees Rhoda, "the John Henry of salvage."

"You loaned me his biography, Professor." Manny winks, throws the blanket over his shoulders, and stands and tests his balance.

She helps him to the bathroom.

"So what's the secret?" he asks once he returns.

"I found some of his personal letters addressed to Carobeth Laird, who was still his wife then. They were never mailed. There are two different caches of paper, in fact. All of historical value. I believe we have a way to ball up Hannity and the Alliance, stop the developers, maybe. Are you well enough?"

"Shipshape, Captain," he waves off her assistance and salutes. "An old salt reporting for duty, what's the poop?" He looks close and adds, "We were lucky before because of the kids."

"I'm counting on you," she agrees.

13

ACROSS FROM RHODA'S room—out of earshot by the garden, Molca's playing cat-and-mouse.

After he left Doc Manny and Juanito to round the knoll, shattered glass crunched underfoot. The overhead security lamps were dark, probably busted out. And something was thrashing the plants below.

Several residents shouted out of the windows, "They're right there. Two of them!"

Everything went quiet.

But with a scrap moon there's little to see. So his radar ears creep forward.

Although the residents switch on the lights in their rooms, shadows outside hide the footing. Sprinting up the grassy hill is a bad idea. The concrete cofferdam waits like a grave. Months ago, Doc Manny donated money for a garden sculpture celebrating the birds, but before the pedestal for the art piece and the fountain itself could be installed, his funds were diverted for publicity to save the shelter. Now that the fountain's on hold, there's just a cement hole in the ground blocked off by construction sawhorses. The sculpture itself is still in the works.

"Get those bastards," someone shouts from the dorms as the vandals sprint away. "There, by the plants."

Tennis shoes slap the ground as two felons sprint for an exit, one toward the gym and the other up the knoll where Molca waits.

Safety barriers or not, the nearest intruder crashes through the caution lamps and pitches head down. His pumpkin skull thuds loud against the cement-lined vault.

Molca hurries over and shines down the light on his key chain. For a moment, nothing moves in the funeral box, and Guzmán almost yells for help. But just then, the intruder turns his face to breathe.

"Damn, E Flat, you wrecked the garden," Guzmán mutters.

Jerrod Cornyn, *alias* E Flat, comes up singing a riff from the Doobie Brothers, "Jesus is just all right with me, oh yeah." Before Jerrod's troubles with fame and his slide to the bottom, he was a roadie with an indie rock band.

"Get out of there," Molca orders the woozy turncoat down in the pit. "You just ate at our table. This is thanks? Why piss on your own bed?"

"I don't like vegetables, reverend, especially fresh." Jerrod, who's seeing double, assumes that the parson's scolding him. He clambers out of the hole using his elbows and knees. Guzmán makes him lie down and checks for a concussion. E Flat's bleeding from a gash on his forehead, and his lower lip is split.

"That's for fruits," E Flat complains as Guzmán's beam searches his pupils. "Charity for fruits and nuts." And then he sings like a rock star, "'My eye, eye Lord, I really want to see You, Lord.'"

"You're stoned and loaded, but thank your thick skull," interrupts Molca. "Call an ambulance," he tells security. "No police!"

Several residents mill around, cursing.

"Anybody see anything?" Molca asks.

Just then, Silvio backs out of the shadows. "No one saw nothing, Sancho," he sneers. "It's too dark."

"That shithead E Flat," someone hisses from the crowd.

"Robbing our food!" a dirt clod smacks Jerrod, no matter that he's bleeding.

"You were standing right there, Silvio, all the while," Guzmán presses. "And you didn't see nothing!"

"Just rolled up on the scene," Silvio spits on the ground, "heard the commotion, came over. I'm sure he can't recall zip with that bump on his head," he points. "Bet he sues."

Molca waves over to security and repeats "no police." *Get everyone back in their rooms,* he thought, *stowaways and ringers might try to slip past.* He glares at Silvio but says nothing. Guzmán borrows a halogen flashlight from a guard so that he can survey the damage.

The tomato vines have been ripped out, but the fruit was just harvested for sauce. A row of pole beans is lost. Several squash plants are uprooted, but the gourds can be cooked for a meal. The vandals even thought to bring gloves, though they dropped them as they fled.

"Food for poor people!" Guzmán exclaims to himself. "Why let them starve?"

"Pissed off everyone, that's what I think," Silvio sneaks up on him. "Preaching the Bible while he divorces his wife!"

"Why tear up a garden so no one can eat?" Guzmán fumes.

"Run him out!" Silvio snickers. "One less phony priest."

The outside floodlamp flashes on again. A security bulb has been replaced.

"Jesus, Silvio, where will these people go?" he asks while the folk are being escorted up the knoll. "They're us."

"Listen, Sancho, if your King of the Sidewalks really cares, then resign. For everyone's good, join these losers!"

"This is the only shelter in the Stingaree," replies Guzmán. "He's trying to keep it open!"

"So he can lord it over us," Silvio replies. "Pretending to be so holy. My feet are white as his."

"Your hair is nappy, Silvio, like mine. Quit trying to pass. What matters is your son. Stop the train, and let him off."

"I might be the town drunk," Silvio sneaks an uppercut. "But at least that kid is mine."

And Guzmán flinches at the remark because of the son he lost, Tizoc. He stoops down and retrieves an acorn squash from an uprooted bush. Until his nemesis leaves, Molca continues salvaging vegetables.

The ambulance hauls E Flat away, and the residents are escorted back to their rooms. And although quiet returns and the lights are back on, Guzmán feels sick. E Flat didn't question why he wrecked the place. Someone told him to do it, and he followed orders. That sort of knee-jerk thinking haunts Molca.

Torn plants litter the ground, bloody bandages too. Fog straggles in from seaward—hazy rainbows clang from the lamps, wringing cold beads from the mist. An unmoored feeling sits him down hard.

Maybe you and E Flat are doubles, he guesses, *all mean, no judgment!* Molca's insulted Doc with his name-calling. Not Doc personally, but friends of Doc that Molca branded not man enough.

And a story comes to mind that the padre told him, a *mea culpa*. It's a confession from a Church Father who stole pears as a boy. Remorse haunts the elder for raiding the orchard, which he did not because he was hungry, not for need or any reason, but simply because of the fence.

Remember Youth Authority, Guzmán flashes back in time, *that prison for minors. Recall that new ward of the court, the quiet kid who kept to himself and who was taunted for it. And you made his life miserable, just like the others who called him a queer. But no one told you to bully him. No one forced you. You nearly shanked him with that bedspring shiv, except that three toughs jumped him first in the exercise yard and broke his jaw. You even made fun as the paramedics wheeled him out. There you were concealing a weapon, which you honed on the concrete deck until it drew blood.*

So the question is not about E Flat and who sent him to tear up the plants, Molca figures. *The point is about you and how you repaid Doc's friendship.*

And Molca muses, *When I was Juanito's age, I wanted to run away from home and school and Shelltown. Live somewhere else. Escape and do better. And yet in jail I bullied that kid just because he preferred men.*

Habits of mind forge a chain. Where's the mental stamp marked "cancel"? No wonder Rhoda keeps to herself, smart as she is. Difference, not truth, is her teacher. And Guzmán marvels that she probably considers him a close-minded thug.

Guzmán's own mother, Florencia, sells tamales for a few pennies profit a piece, instead of making her own from scratch and pocketing the price. So she's stuck being poor. He hates the sight.

Molca's told her, "Get off your knees." But look at the shiftless *huevon* that she married. Who can make tamales to sell when the kitchen's not safe?

Guzmán surveys the garden, breathes in the mist, and worries. Knives are out downtown, it's obvious because of the violence. Got to warn the preacher about the danger; E Flat was a sign. Molca's betting that Lyle Carson and the redevelopment committee have hatched a new plot. Doc's town meeting derailed their agenda, and the meter's running.

We better change our game plan, muses the flyweight, *switch to southpaw or go down in flames. Lead with the left, slip inside their guard. Storm them by surprise. Trouble is Doc's the one with ideas, and he's taken ill.*

14

IN RHODA'S ROOM at the shelter, despite the late hour, she's explaining to Doc Manny how the Register of Historic Places could save the Settlement. Once a site is listed, the law grants certain protections to preserve it for posterity. A monument is not to be razed, ever. Rhoda explains the application forms and ticks off the requirements. The most important is a spot's historical and cultural value. With those elusive specifications in mind, she begins her qualifying exams. He's the examiner.

Point one: Harrington's lost research includes traditional native songs and ancient legends and myths. These are uncollected, found nowhere else. Moreover, his science is illuminated by his unmailed letters to Carobeth, the most personal glimpses of the man himself, unseen until now.

Point two: Europe inspired the legend of Professor Victor Frankenstein whose manic research resurrects the dead. The Americas have John Peabody Harrington who preserved the lifeways of American Indians when many tribes were virtually extinct. Here is the New World's version of death. Rhoda holds up Harrington's biography.

As a human being, moreover, the linguist and anthropologist bats zero. Despite his sense of mission, perhaps because of it, his life careers out of balance. Labeled a crank by academicians, Harrington's obsession with salvage was the butt of jokes at Washington headquarters. He pursued his informants into the furthest backcountry while he lived out of his flivver, sleeping under the car at times. His expenses included cheap rations for them, boiled beef especially, which he ate himself. He rarely published or attended conferences. He feared that other anthropologists would steal his work, so he lived like a hermit, a modern antihero.

At this juncture, Dr. Reese puts up a hand and sits on the bed.

Rhoda's final point is that Harrington lived in this city and taught college classes in Balboa Park. And as luck has it, Rhoda's downtown archeology project with the artifacts *in situ*, confirm how waves of immigrants displaced the First People. The history of settlement is plain, which makes the shelter a prime location for a small museum.

And the old man growls, "Call it a 'museum' and people think of fossils."

"We need to set up a Harrington exhibit," she counters. "We already feature the dig. Let's put up a one-person show."

"Think like a promoter," he muses. "Leak news about 'priceless documents' and 'one-of-a-kind treasures.' That'll fire the cauldron. Local tribes, city fathers, your university, the government. They'll go after each other. That should buy time."

"So what else?" wonders Rhoda.

"We highlight the families and kids, make the shelter real to folk," he advises. "Show them admiring the Harrington things, despite their tough luck with being homeless. Sunnyside up looks good on the plate."

And he points round her room to the carrying baskets and ceremonial drums and the like. "Turn up Charles Dickens—but bright colors. Then we pitch for preserving the past!"

And Rhoda nods at the "we." He's on board with the plan.

"The longer we're news, the better chance to stay put," she seconds.

"Highlight Harrington's wife," Manny suggests. "While he's away doing research, Carobeth's screwing George Laird, a Chemehuevi blacksmith who was supposed to help with translation. Tabloid journals feast on that stuff. What about a reality-show poking fun at cuckolds?"

"Celebrity gossip, that's the new humanism," Rhoda sighs, not sure if he's joking. "Fashion experts and lifestyle pundits on every channel."

Manny snorts and snaps his fingers.

Rhoda wraps up her case for applying to the Register of Historic Places. Now she has to ask him to help. A site isn't safe from developers simply because it's old. An entrepreneur can buy a monument and offer his version of what best serves the common good. Why not a shopping mall instead of an ancient cemetery. Bring in the bulldozers.

Rhoda tries a different argument about using archeology laws to stall for time. Her initial survey of the Harrington cache is positive. Sorting the stuff, however, requires an army. (Consider that a crew of her graduate students already spent months on the dig. And she brought a local shaman and elders on board.) Investigating Harrington's trove will require experts from many different fields. Tribal elders and American Indian scholars, anthropologists, linguists, archeologists, handwriting experts, artifact conservators, among the army.

Her point is that both federal and state policy require authenticating the site, which means two sets of lawyers. Separate agencies will have to sort out jurisdiction and decide who makes decisions. The paperwork alone will bog down the courts.

Doc groans from firsthand experience with petitioning for records.

Who foots the bill for the labor and costs, the legal fees especially? Rhoda presses on. Applying to the register makes the Settlement a petitioner for the common weal, not a litigant. So it shouldn't be sued for costs. Who pays then: the feds, the state, or the private donors?

Manny reminds her that jurisdiction and fees aren't the only obstacles. Both the Alliance of Churches and her university already have gone to court. James Hannity alleges that Steve "arbitrarily" decides who to let in to the shelter, including noncitizens.

The college, meanwhile, is suing the mission for breach of contract because it won't allow classes on the premises. Yet research has been ongoing for many semesters. Also, the college alleges discrimination, but on the basis of religion not race. The shelter lets in Christians but restricts academics.

Rhoda offers her own take on legal matters. Involve the politicians since they crave the limelight. Let legislators shake out their egos.

"And while the lawmakers grandstand for the press," Doc agrees, "the case goes nowhere. Your dig proceeds unimpeded. The artifacts remain on site."

"That's my hope," Rhoda admits.

"What's in it for you?" Doc Manny asks, as if she's being deposed for a trial.

"I get to publish the results of my research."

"No good deed goes unpunished," he warns. "Archeology's a business. We need legal guidance at the state and federal levels. Building our gym required tons of forms.

"Your plan's risky," he continues, "all those applications and waivers. But sometimes paper stops a train." He wraps the blanket close.

She watches from the recliner chair guessing it's about three in the morning. "How are you feeling?"

He waves off the question and checks on his briefcase. Usually, he's the one who asks how she's doing.

"You can check the registry on the computer," she lowers her voice with Juanito snoring. "The applications are ready to send," she adds.

"Okay," Doc replies. "Right now, though, I'm beat. Am I keeping you up?" he eyes the bed.

Her insomnia goes unmentioned.

"Do you have the stomach for this fight?" he stretches out.

"We succeeded before," replies Rhoda, harking back to their campaign against city hall. "Why not now?"

"We'll have to get down in the mud. But that's politics." Manny rubs his palms together for warmth.

"What about you, Doctor?" she replies. "Ready?"

He gestures at his briefcase, "there's my answer. I'll fight as long as I can."

"I cleaned up your suit," Rhoda says, trying to hide her feelings by smoothing his coat on a hanger.

"You'll be headlining this rematch, topping the marquee," he says out of the blue. "Just remember your promise, Professor. Don't let them sweep me under the grass," he murmurs. "The military drove me out. A potter's field beats government ground."

And Rhoda swallows and nods—imagines her mother at the hospital waiting alone for the dark.

"Now, the padre," offers Manny, taking his cue from her silence, "he believes in redeeming souls. I stick to medicine. No doctor has a prescription for kindness."

"The Settlement must seem strange." He takes a sip of water. "The way we talk, like a storm's coming. Ideas are your wheelhouse; comebacks used to be mine."

"The suit looks fine," the doctor says. He smoothes the pleats. "When Molca gets back, I'll shine my shoes. My kit is in his closet. Did you know that his parents live a few miles away?" the old man lies back in the bed, arms at his sides. "But Molca hardly visits. Can't. Doors close, you move on. In the military, your post changes, and so does the world. There's Punctuated Equilibrium for you," he jokes about a sidebar corollary to Darwin's theory of evolution when change happens fast.

Rhoda chuckles despite her wet cheeks, because they're back to science. "Tough exam," she remarks. "Do I get the diploma?"

The old man rubs his forehead and smiles like the Buddha.

15

"*ORALE*, GLADYS!" OUT on the streets, in front of the mission, Guzmán recognizes a working girl that the Settlement tried once to rescue from her pimp. "Up late, *chica*. It's chilly tonight."

"Keep me warm?" she pops her gum. "Wanna play doctor?"

"I'm in training," he replies, on a trek to warn the priest about the raid. "You hear the racket tonight?"

"Scared away business," she yawns.

"E Flat tore up the plants. Seen anything yourself?"

"You got money to pay?" Gladys fires back. "Charity's for Sunday mass."

"Me, I'm heathen," Guzmán responds. "But the priest's done right by us. And now someone wrecks the garden. Not from need, just spite. They're up to something. But don't bother yourself."

"Why come off so righteous?" she flares. "A meal and a flop and 'thank you, Jesus.'"

"Me, holy?" he yucks at himself. "No religion, bad judgment." He can't help laughing. "Think of it. You're nothing but right! Do a good deed," he snorts. "For what?"

"Oh, I do you good, but mojo ain't free," the young woman turns in profile.

Guzmán turns out his pockets and shakes his hips.

"Okay," she laughs at the sight, chafing her arms from the cold, "Who smashed Eden, you think?" Molca's supposed to be smart. Everyone knows that he's going to college, this beat-up ex-boxer, the maître d' at Chez Lunch-a-Lot.

"The city wants the property," he tells her, "the college too, and throw in the Alliance of Churches."

"They're all the same John," she replies. "They need a bad girl like me."

"Meaning what?" he asks her.

"Circle jerk," she answers flashing a palm, "getting themselves off. No matter their bullshit about progress, bulldozing flowers is hand-jive."

"Some people knock down a tree cuz it's there," she explains. "Down in the mud, everybody's dirty. Anything goes. Nobody's better, which is boring. That's why they pay Gladys to die for their sins."

"Welcome to church, *profeta*!" He brings both fists to his chest. "Good tidings and all." Molca resumes walking. *Saint Steve*, he thinks, *you listening to this prophet?*

A block down Broadway, across from TransPac Commercial, three men flank the sidewalk shoulder to shoulder. Molca jaywalks the street, sidestepping the sporadic car. But they do the same—two in sprints with their hands in their pockets, and the other in leather striding a half pace in front.

Guzmán loiters under a streetlamp.

"Hey, homes, what's your set?" the lean one named *Tuerto* with the teardrop tattoos steps in Molca's way.

"I'm from the Settlement," replies Guzmán. "We've met."

Guzmán turns to the welterweight sporting the slick calfskin coat. "Is that you, *Cuco*? How about a good word?" Guzmán points with his chin to *Tuerto*.

"Easy, *Tuerto*," the leader calms his *carnal*. "We shoot hoops with this *vato*. Molca works with Padre Steve and that sharp *judío* doctor, the ex-promoter Manny Reese. Your cousin joined his boxing club."

Tuerto pumps fists with Guzmán, which eases the tension. "My *padrino* might be dropping by," the homeboy announces. "Corcoran gave him an early release. But no one's hiring *pintos* out of the joint."

The dude to *Tuerto's* left paws with his foot as if losing patience. Molca doesn't know his name. Is he a brother or Afro-Hispano? Molca can't decide. He's never seen him at the gym.

"Heard the city's tearing down the mission," *Cuco* checks the street up and down.

"Trying," Guzmán confirms, worried about the new *cholo* with the bulge in his jacket who won't talk. Molca keeps the lamppost between them.

"You had more trouble tonight," *Cuco* mentions.

"Why smash up a garden?" replies Guzmán. "Heard anything?"

"Maybe the *gavachos* trashed the place to run you out," *Cuco* shrugs, "except that Silvio's a twisted *cabron* who carries a grudge. So you tell us."

Just then, in the blink of an eye, the trio duck into an alley.

A flashing black and white patrol car screeches up under the streetlamp. The curbside door flings open as a uniform yells, "Stop, you ragheads!"

"Let them go!" the driver orders as he dismounts from the vehicle. The cop approaches Guzmán with his hand on his holster. He's not a big man, but he's wearing a badge.

"How's our favorite angel of mercy?" asks the patrol sergeant.

"Officer Dexter, how'd ja' doo!" Guzmán jives and places both hands on the roof of the car.

As Sergeant Dexter pats him down, he tells his training partner, "We frisk for weapons. That's policy. Doesn't matter who. The court's all hot for gun owners' rights. We assume everyone's carrying. Molca there works at the Settlement, He's Padre Steve's assistant."

The new rookie pretends to pull the pin on a fragmentation grenade and roll it inside an enemy fortress.

"Nah," the sergeant responds to the former soldier, "Molca's a 'friendly.' You never heard of 'winning hearts and minds'?"

And the newbie smirks, "Yeah, right," and slaps his holster.

"Hold on, rookie," replies the sergeant, "Here's a tip. Quite a few of you former sandtroopers bed down on the sidewalks. Returning home doesn't take—you're lost in transit, sort of. The shelter offers a flop and a meal. The cooking's not bad."

And he turns to Molca and asks, "Where you headed?"

"The padre's on site buffing the Ashton Office Suites. I'm due there."

"Lucky for you Sergeant Milkin's off tonight," the officer tells him. "He'd kick your huddled masses down the road."

"That concludes the field stop," Officer Dexter switches over to the new hire with the nameplate O'Connor. "Got it?"

And then the patrol supervisor signals the new recruit to stand guard by the car and walks Guzmán out of earshot. "Heard you had trouble tonight," Sergeant Dexter tells Guzmán where they can't be overheard.

"Couple of vandals tore up the garden."

"Smart move not to call 911," the cop tells Molca. "Someone upstairs wants to bring in the swat team. Dial up more bad publicity. Run you out."

Guzmán's already been informed.

"How's my nephew?" Officer Dexter covers his mouth to inquire. The other cop's watching.

JOE RODRÍGUEZ

"Doc Manny got him another consult at the veteran's hospital," replies the ex-flyweight, pretending to tie his boxing shoes. "Three tours of combat don't go away, especially disabled. He works fine in the laundry, though."

"Quiet up here," deadpans the police sergeant, who drills an index finger into his skull and saunters down range.

"How about a ride?" Molca falls back into character, a court jester spoofing the Sheriff of Nottingham, street clown to badge. King Arthur and the Round Table took the day off. "The Ashton's not far," Molca japes.

"Sure, slick," Officer Dexter taps the logo on the car, *Protect and Serve*. "Only a chauffeur's not included. Hard enough teaching junior here how to play by the book."

16

IN THE HUB of the downtown financial district, out back of the Ashton Office Suites, is a chromed trapdoor elevator designed for ferrying supplies and equipment to a service tunnel that leads to the basement. An access port accepts ID cards. Once a plastic pass is inserted, the gleaming doors fold up and out of the way as the platform ascends to ground level, ready for loading. Janitors, utility workers, repair technicians, and plumbers stick to that entrance. The Ashton's tenants, including legal firms and stockbrokers, defense contractors, and engineering consultants, stride through the front. At this late hour, that main street portal is locked.

As Guzmán heads for the chromed lift, a scant crescent moon finds its aim. Wrought-iron sidelamps burnish the quicksilver walkway. Something scuttles across the tinted concrete into a hedge.

At the rear of the skyscraper, no loading dock clutters the architect's lines—the pretense is perfect. The Ashton was built by theme park developers used to hiding the guts of a fantasy palace. Retractable security gates, electro-painted to match the vaulting parapets, protect and disguise the loading platforms. Nearby, a three-ton heating and cooling substation hums within a trim lattice kiosk. Behind the walls of the main building, soundproof maintenance corridors complete the illusion of no moving parts.

So where is the Settlement's beat-up van? Guzmán worries. After the raid at the mission, he needs to see for himself.

The shelter's vehicle turns up in service lot D, under a sodium lightpost. And there is a problem: the old buggy lists like a sinking ship. Before Guzmán approaches the right rear wheel, he checks the surroundings in case of an ambush, wraps one hand in a bandanna as he sweeps wide. And true to suspicion, the tire's rubbing strip has been slashed through to the radial ply, despite the security patrols and surveillance cameras.

After Guzmán checks the other three treads, he jogs to the service elevator and inserts his key card in the access port. Something's on, and he has a guess—the vandals are due for another visit.

The heavy doors whisk open and close; the platform descends.

Down below, as he navigates the warren of bright fluorescent tunnels, the whitewashed ducts, cables, and pipes muffle his passage. Although office folk are working on the other side of the wall, he hears nothing. The white light makes it hard to see, like an alien spaceship. But there's no time to adjust. As he zoomed round a tight corner and headed for an elevator, a blurry giant jumps in the way.

"Whoa," the creature grunts. Guzmán almost fires a left hook. "Is that you, Molca?" a voice asks.

"Damn, Padre, sound your horn. I almost clipped you!"

"You okay, Mr. G?" returns Steve. "Something jumped out of the light. I keep hoping . . . ," he says. The padre's been praying for a sign. "I'm on my way to bring the van around," Steve covers his mouth and yawns. "The crew is upstairs closing shop."

"There was some trouble at the mission," Guzmán informs him.

"We figured bad news when you didn't show," replies Steve. "And your cellphone wasn't picking up. Tell me outside."

"Hold a minute," Guzmán pauses. "Trouble might have followed me here. A tire's been slashed."

"There's a spare in the van and a jack," the padre answers.

"Vandals trashed the garden tonight. The cut tire's no coincidence."

"Is everyone safe?"

"Don't worry," Guzmán tells him. "There's no fire." He's not mentioning Doc Manny's condition nor the burial promise. Not right now.

"Let's go," the priest steps toward the door.

"Anything strange happen tonight?" Molca interrupts.

"Brother James dropped by. The Alliance wants me to switch sides. And Lyle Carson paid us a visit, remember. You think it's him causing trouble?"

"The two of them," Molca pauses. "Bad mix."

The padre rushes for the exit.

"Not so fast," Guzmán advises.

Outside, Steve checks the slashed rubber, retrieves the jack, and sets to work. "This was personal," he remarks as he frees a lug nut. The van's logo for Angel Clean has been gouged down to the metal.

Molca slaps away a moth—he himself dreamed up the name. Angel Clean fits the business and leads in the phonebook. Tonight, though, Satan's on speed dial!

Molca fetches the spare tire. They work fast. And just as Steve pops the hubcap back on, a car rolls up with guys in ski masks.

"Hit hard," Guzmán barks, thrusts a pry bar at the priest, and crouches at the ready. Without a word, three assailants jump out with knives: two charge at Molca; the other charges at the minister.

Molca ducks low under the first slasher's reach and batters his knee with the jack handle. The intruder yelps and goes down, clutching his leg. His partner tries to slice Guzmán's face. The ex-boxer parries—by just inches. He slams the thug's ribs, first with one end of the metal shaft, then the other, like a riot baton. Both hits crunch bone. A loose blade skitters across asphalt.

The padre's not so lucky. His left bicep is cut and bloody, yet he wields the pry bar like a broadsword, trying to hold off the intruder, whose right arm hangs limp.

Just then, Becky and Reza from the cleaning crew dash out of the building screaming at the masked thugs. Reinforcements turn the tide, even though only two of the workers intervene.

The crippled assassins escape in the car, almost running down the cavalry.

"The padre's bleeding," Becky yells and stanches his wound with a cleaning towel.

"A doctor can sew you up, Padre," Guzmán says as he examines the cut. A tourniquet isn't necessary, but just barely since an artery's close. And he breathes deep of the cool night air realizing that they have to act fast. Time to switch southpaw, stop playing defense.

"Doc Manny's with Rhoda," Molca whispers and pats Steve's back. And then Guzmán announces out loud, "Those creeps had box cutters. What respect they show!"

By now, the entire crew has quit hiding and run to the scene. "This is crazy," Fred stutters.

"That's quits for me, Padre," Molca shouts for effect. "Combat pay's not included. Your arm's wrecked. I'm not Rahab, and you're not Joshua." That Bible story is about sending spies to win a battle. The minister should figure out that Molca's up to something.

And Guzmán flings away the jack handle and stalks away. Pretending to switch sides isn't farfetched. *Am I jumping ship or faking a defection?* If Molca weren't so jealous about Rhoda, he wouldn't doubt motives.

Becky calls him back while applying pressure to the pastor's wound.

"Let him go," utters Steve, confused by Guzmán's antic disposition. Why mention Rahab and Joshua from the Old Testament? Is his right hand speaking in code?

Guzmán, meanwhile, turns tail like Judas. *But I make this stink to draw in flies,* he tells himself.

Two times tonight the shelter's been a target. Lyle Carson appears, and the garden's wrecked. Then Hannity shows, and there's an ambush. Carson, though, was married to Rhoda, which makes his involvement personal.

I'll play the traitor to find out her ex-husband, Molca decides. *I'll go to his campus office in person. My bad reputation he trusts.*

The cleaning crew, meanwhile, rushes the padre back to the Settlement and rouses Doc Manny from his sickbed.

There at the infirmary, Doc Manny shoos everyone out while he washes out the wound, sews Steve up, and shoots him full of antibiotics. Bloody bandages fill an emesis basin. A surgical kit is torn open. Doc's one of the best cut-men in the business, ill or not.

A tetanus shot is insurance against lockjaw.

Why maim a minister with a knife? Rhoda and Juanito are baffled. As for Molca's desertion, not on your life. Juanito looks up to the man. And with Silvio in the picture, Rhoda guesses that something's up, some sort of trick.

Steve, though, offers no explanation for Molca's treachery—in fact, just repeats, "You know Molca—do you trust him?" So the boy holds up his head and yet wanders through the gym, grasping the ropes as if he's adrift.

With Molca missing, everyone has to work harder. The shelter feeds a hundred people, at least, three meals a day. The rolls keep growing. Preparations begin before dawn. After a hot breakfast, a clean sweep is necessary, fore and aft. Each resident is assigned a task. (There's barely time to reset the clock before the next tide floods at mid-afternoon.) Check-out goes at one.

So please pitch in, residents. Or city inspectors might swoop down in white gloves and shut down the place. Once your area passes inspection, proceed to the cafeteria and have a seat. Chez Lunch-a-Lot thanks you.

And after the noon clean up once the kitchen sparkles, this window of time is when the padre calls together Rhoda, Manny, and the boy. Since Juanito's upset, it's best to keep him close, school notwithstanding. The adults can let off steam. The boy can't, He's liable to wander away. The best he can do is sit quietly.

So they assemble at a kitchen counter, off by themselves, which is nothing unusual. Changing routine will fire up gossip, especially today. The group gathers at a back corner, with an extra dessert for the kid.

Strict privacy, though, isn't necessary because the minister censors himself in the pantry. "I'm not sure what happened at the Ashton," he offers, which is barely downwind from a lie. Molca stormed away, sure. But might he return like the cavalry, despite his own demons? He spoke in code about sneaking behind enemy lines to find out who's sabotaging the shelter. Find that out, and the long odds might even.

Tangled—all so tangled. Who knows what's coming or from where, but you can bet the Lord's not in it. The padre doesn't invite Manny and Rhoda to join with him and pray, because doubt and uncertainty are how they think. The parson's own arm was just nicked to the bone despite Molca's coaching. *Slide, glide, and tenderize* didn't ward off Old Nick.

Days before what happened at the Ashton, the minister practiced how to sidestep an assailant's knife, duck to the inside, and whack him in the skull. When the assault occurred, how he was tempted to kill! Only God's hand switched his aim so that he bruised Satan's shoulder merely. "Turn the other cheek" happened by accident. An "eye for an eye" was intended.

How can a minister devise a homily about wanting to murder someone and forget the reason or cause? The notion of grace under fire doesn't fit the crime.

As for Rhoda, finding a moment of quiet has to wait. There's her mother to care for. Oh, add the three others at the kitchen table with her. Scholarship is welcome. Her hunch that baskets and pottery connect with the origins of writing. With that she could theorize about how the alphabet preserves human memory across generations. People who read about the past need not repeat the same mistakes.

Which comes first, she wonders, *symbols (some birds can count)—or minds fit for language?* Weaving grass baskets or sculpting mud into pottery requires instruction and how-to diagrams. A shared culture distributes this shorthand guide that might develop into print, the next step in evolution. Otherwise, people begin at zero each generation, and nothing changes.

The question, though, is what good did insights about cultures far different from his own do Harrington? This genius was cut off while obsessed with lost tribes. Science inspired his devotion, not making a home! Dressing for company begins when we're alone. Set another place for dinner. His letters to Carobeth mouldered in secret.

Yet shouldn't someone obsessed with the grave be open to change? Transformation is a sort of death because the old self has to go. Yet Harrington can't turn around and start from scratch.

Rhoda glances around the kitchen table, and she's tempted to laugh. She has to stage an exhibit right away to help keep the shelter open. She's nowhere near cataloguing Harrington's stuff. The science isn't close to 100 percent.

Behind her the dishwasher, who lost his his farm to a drug cartel, scrapes burnt caramel from baking trays.

Doc Manny, Rhoda recalls, just gave Juanito a Roadrunner T-shirt from the comic convention. Why not a bulletproof vest, now that the garden's turning into trench warfare? Birds eat each other but don't scorch the earth!

Such thoughts as these are winging around the kitchen table.

"Yes, we're all worried about Molca," the padre admits. "Yet together, each one, we can pick up the slack."

"That's Molca's talent—covering our backs," Doc offers.

"Molca's our champ," pipes up Juanito.

"The best," the priest affirms, "but for now, we carry the ball ourselves. Together, though, we can do it." He pats the boy's shoulder and says, "Protect each other." Satan's name is isolation, but he doesn't say that.

"One other thing," Rhoda speaks up. "I found old boxes of research papers hidden here at the Settlement, stuff left by John Peabody Harrington probably, a famous scientist. I meant to tell you, I didn't know how. I'm sorry." She nods at Doc Manny whom she's already told.

"I need all your help to set up an exhibit here. Our small museum. And soon."

"Harrington, yes," rejoins Steve. "Juanito told me."

"Juanito?" she repeats.

"I did a bad thing," the boy murmurs, head bowed. The name John Peabody Harrington had come up before. So Juanito opened Rhoda's computer to find out more about him. But after the youngster dialed up the name, his best friend Molca vanishes. Just so, when Juanito's father Silvio doesn't come home, the boy must be at fault. Monsters do bad even not trying.

"You taught the kid how to use the Internet," Steve reminds Rhoda. "And after he searched the web, he asked me if I met the guy." The minister chuckles, "Am I that old?"

Rhoda's not amused.

"Sorry," the preacher adds. "Harrington had a habit of hiding his stuff. So I figured a cache turned up here. Don't be angry."

"Let's go easy on each other," Doc Manny shrugs. "There's a lot to make right. Redemption starts late, if you live long enough."

"You can't imagine," she seconds.

Rhoda assures the boy that he didn't hurt anyone. However, she'll clear her desk and hide everything. What other surprises are in the works?

All Juanito hears is Rhoda's tone. He's done bad, again. "Love is as love does," that's how she acts.

Before closing their meeting, Steve asks to join hands for a moment of silence. Rhoda welcomes making amends. Trust has been shaken, and not just with Molca.

For the padre this moment is despair, *the sickness unto death*, which encompasses more than Regina and God.

Not one resident advised their pastor to be on guard, although someone heard rumblings of trouble, surely. Consider that many pray at the chapel. So where's the gospel in practice? Yes people are frail, but please, where's the simple care for each other? Warn your minister!

Steve already has posted a notice that he was injured on the job—not for the first time, he reminds folk. That's supposed to be a joke, a wink for the good. Why announce that he's been waylaid and cut? Everyone stays calm. Earlier that day, Rhoda had retrieved Steve's bloody shirt from the infirmary, plus the surgical linens, and carried the lot to the laundry where she washed them herself.

With so many earthquakes already, she has to close her eyes. Doc Manny volunteers to stay with Juanito so that she can go to her room and rest. Those two can talk about computer stuff and comic books and the convention downtown. Then he'll walk the boy home.

After Rhoda leaves the kitchen meeting and returns to her room, she uploads an announcement via computer about her Harrington discovery. Uncertainty becomes real once she presses the "send" button because all hell will break loose. Chaos is more than a mathematical concept with Harrington in the equation. Will his papers provoke interest in the museum, particularly here in town? The unmailed letters to Carobeth could draw a crowd because people are people, and they love to pry. The more publicity, the better it is for the mission.

The Settlement's application to the Register of Historic Places, let it be noted, already has been submitted.

17

THE NEXT MORNING, after Rhoda showers, does her hair and dresses, a knock rattles her door. Without thinking, she unbars the latch. Her department chair, Professor Ernst (Ernie) Spiller, steps inside as if late for an appointment.

"Forgive my intrusion," he smiles, but with a countinghouse edge—loose bills need sorting, so let's get to it. Usually, he dispenses geniality like house mints, this chair for fifteen years.

"Excuse me," Rhoda steps back, a bit late for caution. Too close and her skin crawls. He anchors himself at the threshhold.

"Let me come to the point, Rhoda. We're all busy." Having to sign in with security out-front hones his sharp edge. "Withdraw that request that the Settlement be declared a historic landmark. Protected status ties the university's hands. We can't build on the property. We lose funding and grant money."

"But the paperwork's been filed," she responds. How did the college find out so fast?

"Have the reverend rescind the nomination to the register," replies Chair Spiller, with his sallow satyr's smile. "For right now, let Harrington's files and letters stay put. We can negotiate later." Ernie's pale fingers squeeze the folder under his arm. His work's not outside in the field anymore.

"All Parson Bentham has to do is sign this letter of withdrawal," the chair urges, as he extracts the prepared document. "I'll deliver a copy to the administration."

"What do I tell Steve?" she asks. The university letterhead is not to be trusted, especially when Rhoda's ex-husband owes his job to the college.

Spiller's nose wrinkles as if from gas fumes. He extends the papers again. "Tell him the truth: that withdrawing is in your best interest."

"My interest, why mine?" she counters.

"Your notification about the Harrington find is late. The provost can fire you for malfeasance," he warns.

"But Harrington has nothing to do with the dig. That discovery is my own."

"Anything you do is on university time. They own our science."

Rhoda returns to her desk. Professor Spiller holds out the letter. "Listen, Rhoda, how many years before you retire: ten, fifteen? File a contract grievance if you want. But win or lose, there won't be time for the lab anymore. Putting out fires will suck you dry. Tenure won't protect you."

"What happened to us, Ernie?" she turns to face him. "A century ago, people sacrificed an orchard to build this college. Now we grind out diplomas like cars. Professors aren't colleagues; we're petty Machiavels brandishing résumés."

"Please, Professor Bart," the chair sighs. "Why do students take a degree, wisdom, or a cushy job? Poll your classes." He plops down the withdrawal letter and weights it with a pen. "Why lose your best years? Buck the provost, and you'll teach five hundred at eight o'clock sharp. Half accept creation, not Darwin's science. And their class evaluations wind up on her desk."

Spiller points at Rhoda, shrugs, and leaves.

Rhoda fidgets with a knapped flake of obsidian, then examines some brittle shards from a broken pickling jar and wipes her fingers.

Her mother still applies lotions and balms to moisturize her skin, ill from cancer or not. Empress of the Ordinary, Thelma jokes, as she rubs lanolin from the bottle. Queen of the Mundane.

Rhoda has struggled hard to be more than ordinary, an ordinary woman especially always stuck with the dishes. What if making a home sets the mark for everyone, no matter who they are? The folk at the shelter envy house chores.

Rhoda recalls her mom preparing breakfast before driving to work. After her shift at the docks, she hurried home to prepare dinner, wash dishes, and clean. This was Thelma's schedule, with or without a man of the house.

When Rhoda's step-dad was away at sea, however, she and Thelma took dinner by the television. Their favorites were the original Flash Gordon movie serials from the '30s. Thelma's parents had taken her to the cinema when she was a girl which was a special outing!

As the restored videocasettes flew to Mars, Thelma's laugh spilled over. Rhoda couldn't resist the fun. Rocketships powered by firecrackers. The beautiful Dale Arden beyond helpless with Flash always to the rescue! And Ming the Merciless, the Asian peril, was always plotting to rule the galaxy, stroking his whip mustache as he schemed how to bed her. Only Professor Zarkoff with his wild Einstein hair didn't walk into traps. He stayed busy in the laboratory saving the world.

Who wouldn't covet such brainpower?

And Rhoda recalls the chair's visit, envying when the villains in the movies arrived from outer space. Ernie dropped by to pimp her archeology and the artifacts, which are "intellectual property" meant to bring the university cash.

Now that Rhoda's posted word of the Harrington find, Ernie will bluster, "Get on board with the college foundation or deal with the consequences!" He means Provost Marcie Tarpon, the enforcer.

But Rhoda has a history already with Provost Tarpon, the second-in-command, who advised Rhoda not to file a complaint against Lyle. Rhoda's ex claims a co-written book manuscript as his alone. Rhoda scheduled an appointment in the main office, but only said that it was personal.

Rhoda dressed for battle, down to her jewelry.

Provost Tarpon thumbed through Rhoda's file, straightened her sapphire bracelet, and handed back the folder.

"There's a procedure for copyright infringement, of course, which involves faculty committees and such." Tarpon smiled across her desk. "But you'll wind up biasing the men at all levels. Being right is so unseemly to them.

"Especially after a nasty divorce," the provost added, as she stood and handed back Rhoda's complaint of plagiarism. (Lyle's office is just down the hall from her).

"Self-publish your next book," the provost advised. "Don't wait. Apply for release time; compete for a stipend. My careful consideration, I promise for your post-tenure review."

Rhoda picks up Ernie's recision letter to the Register of Historic Places. If Steve signs it, the shelter loses that opportunity for government protection. Whether he signs the withdrawal notice or not, box-canyon logic has trapped her again. She can't win.

Where is Dr. Zarkoff with his invisibility ray? There's no way now but over the cliff.

Before she tests the edge, she'll brew a cup of tea.

Then the Harrington display goes up!

18

"COME SHARE WITH us, friends," Doc Manny calls out to the garden, as Juanito skips by the grassy knoll.

"They're in their glory this time of day," Manny points to the flock of feathered guests.

What he's applauding, especially, is the memorial fountain that's just been delivered and hauled near the foot of the incline, across from the plants. The stainless-steel wings curving upright on edge, nest metal bowls that will channel water in gentle cascades. Heavy pallets bear the full weight. The job now is to lift the sculpted waterworks onto the cofferdam plinth so that nothing breaks.

The sight lifts their spirits.

The fountain will complement the cover of green close by and the sweeping flights of color.

At least, that's what Manny and the boy see in their minds' eye, although the fountain hasn't yet been lifted into place. The base of the monument, the cofferdam, needs to be filled in before the half-ton or so of metal is muscled a few feet and mounted. The welded alloy and steel has to be centered and plumbed before the dedication.

"The padre says we need water," chimes in the boy, which is correct, but not quite the parson's drift about saving the shelter.

At that moment, someone familiar slouches past, and Manny calls out, "Professor Spiller. We met at the city hall." Manny nods to Rhoda's nemesis, a.k.a. "Herr Ernie" to the mission staff. "Dr. Manfred Reese, Professor." Doc extends his hand to the head of anthropology. "You represented the university before the planning commission. Half of downtown was there to protest. That was just a while ago."

Juanito stops dancing and edges back.

"Your field is archeology, Professor Spiller, if I recall," smiles Manny. "You chair Rhoda's department. Are you here to visit?"

"Her dig is instructive," Spiller buys time, while he tries to recall who this is. "I study how cultures manage war, how they supplant each other by force of arms."

Manny the Hat grins at the man. "Professor Bart's exhibit is worthy, then. Armies marching through and such. Were you ever in the service?"

"Excuse me?" Spiller frowns. He just got it. This loopy old faggot derailed the plans for the stadium.

Doc Manny notices Ernie's red eyes and offers, "Back from a ballgame, Professor?

"I'm sorry?" replies Spiller who misses the tag. He's been drinking.

Juanito turns to run.

"Sports are good for stress," Doc adds. "Nothing's more relaxing than baseball, which is why I prefer birdwatching."

Blinking in the sun, Ernie's blindsided by the physician's wit, his Zen *koan* about clearing the mind.

"That's enough, old man," Ernie replies and quits the field.

"'Do no harm,'" Doc Manny says to the boy, who fetches the commander's famous lawn chair so that he can sit and enjoy the outdoors. Doc doesn't look well, especially after his midnight rescue from the barrio clinic.

"Herr Spiller's eyes do have a yellow tinge," Manny sighs and sits. "And I smelled vodka on his breath. He should worry about jaundice. Besides, he scares the birds."

Doc Manny reaches under the seat to make sure of his briefcase. It's gone!

"Rhoda has it," Juanito pats his shoulder.

And the old man wonders, Will she keep her promise to bury me, no matter what? His left arm's gone numb, and he stretches it out. Molca's given his word too, and so has the padre.

A few weeks ago, after Manny's scheduled chemotherapy treatment, he hemorrhaged blood from the colon. The anticancer agents have side effects like that. He admitted himself to the emergency room, where he was typed and cross-matched, just in case he needed a transfusion. Also, a protonix infusion was administered.

Half conscious on the gurney with IVs running in both arms, Doc needed warm blankets because of the blood loss. The dingy ceiling staggered overhead. The old man felt as if he was present and not present, afraid and unafraid. The beep of the monitors and the flurrying staff barely rippled the canvas.

The Buddhist state of *satori*, the peace that surpasses understanding, might feel just so.

I can do this, he thought, as he joked with epitaphs. Here lies Manny the Hat. Quick hands, late conscience. And a thought leapt to mind. Any Western physician has heard of Galen most likely, the epitome of Roman medicine. Galen treated wounded gladiators in the Colosseum. War taught him his craft.

With that reference to war, time and space became unhinged for Manfred Saul Reese. Instead of lying on a gurney in a civilian hospital, Manny was back aboard a U.S. Navy ship stationed off the Hawaiian Islands.

What was the name of the *kanaka* pig hunter caught downwind by accident during a clandestine weapons test in the jungle? The man almost died aboard Dr. Reese's amphibious helicopter carrier, which was picketed miles offshore. The drugs Doc administered, though, won't let his patient remember. So Doc carries the memory instead. The man had steelwool red hair and freckles, a Polynesian face with mixed features. He was a big *hapa* from the Big Island, *Ho'alu* it was, wasn't it—"Slack the rope." That name also stands for the slack-key guitar, *ho'alu*, the immigrant guitar that revived Hawaiian music. Manny's reminded of the gallows.

Why chase the past? Manny frets, close by the fountain, while a seawind swirls from the coast. Don't alarm the boy who's staring at the toolshed as if something's wrong! Sweat chills the back of Doc's neck. His arm's still numb.

Why can't an old man accept death? The dry water is there.

19

*T*HAT GHOSTY OLD *owl nailed to the roof is not scary like people. And the boy recalls watching Molca spy on Reverend Steve and Rhoda from the kitchen window. The look on his face was like taking a punch. Like blood in the mouth.*

"'Harrington's three-ring circus,'" *Molca muttered in the pantry, while the boy watched. Molca's breath steamed the glass.* "Just like us," *he said. His reflection made fists by his side.*

Mention Harrington's name and all the grown-ups growl at each other.

Spitting words at each other, the grown-ups, smiling or not—like Doc Manny and the other guy beefing just now, that Professor Spiller. Ready to bite. But if they care so much that kids be good, why so noisy themselves? Why so mean to each other?

Are people monsters, all of us?

Everything's wrong all of a sudden. First Manny disappears, then Molca walks out! Someone's arm is cut open in a parking lot; his friends dread the worse.

Where can I hide, get away from people, never come out? Birds own the air, so they sing all they want.

But I have to do something or the shelter's torn down.

The night before last, was it? Padre Steve's cut arm rusted his shirt. That's what I hoped, as he stood in the light. Just a stain. *The worse keeps arriving.*

The cleaning crew woke Doc so he could sew Steve up, and the old man hurried to the infirmary, though he's sick himself. They told me to stay behind in Rhoda's room, but I carried his medical bag.

At the infirmary, Manny said that Steve had to have stitches, and he told everyone to leave. Steve asked him to not cut off the shirt, and he wiggled out of his skin, which he saved. Doc unwrapped a curved needle and dangly white thread before he noticed that I was still there. Rhoda fetched me away. I scrubbed my shoes against the sidewalk and wiped my hands on the grass, as the moon cast shadows on the ground.

When the surgery was over, Steve's arm was bandaged white. A sling stapled his wrist to his chest. When he stood up to leave, his cellphone fell from his pocket. I wanted to keep it so he would be close.

Who cut him? And why did Guzmán leave? Is Molca okay? Why do people say nothing and make us worry?

The boy glances at the fountain and the bare concrete foundation, envying that cofferdam box for the silence.

Rhoda's mad at me, and Padre Steve is cut. "Our three-ring circus," Molca says—I overheard that.

Doc Manny's the one who explains things to me about Molca and Rhoda, and Rhoda and Steve. Doc says: a three-ring circus. You want to know? Your pal Molca means a big circus ring, bub, real fast and noisy with all the hustle and stuff. A three ring circus hits like a speedbag in your chest. Doc Manny straightens my baseball cap as if I bat next. Three weight-classes boxing all at once, he continues. And you're the referee. Wait a few years, champ, and you'll understand. Adults-only kind of stuff.

The boy checks on the Maestro of Wings asleep in his chair. His closed eyes flicker in the shadowy light.

Doc's briefcase is with Rhoda. And the medicine bag. So are Molca's boxing gloves—the ones that smell of the sea.

Sometimes Juanito wishes he were far away as a bird high up. In his mind's eye, as if on a computer screen, he leaps from the fountain and soars at the sun, light as a speck of pollen. Do all monsters fly?

20

ABOUT THE VERY moment that Juanito soars above the fountain, Guzmán has a waking dream about a boy. The ex-flyweight's spent a restless night under a bush at the college because there was nowhere to sleep downtown after he walked out on the shelter's cleaning crew. (Crime is up on campus too. Staying out of sight, though, is Guzmán's nature.)

He has to visit Vice President Lyle Carson, pay him a call, find out who attacked the pastor at the Ashton Business Suites. Someone's out for blood. The administration building, though, is not user friendly for students or visitors. Feels like a courthouse or a jail.

Despite a full blinding sky, Molca's still drowsy. Although he should hurry, he can barely keep his eyes open. Stretched out on the grass beneath a Torrey pine, near the university quad, snippets of memory clatter and jump through his head. An antique movie projector is running too fast to make sense of the plot.

A fence lizard watches Molca from a few feet away, as he in turn watches a kid convert an empty mayonnaise jar into a specimen bottle. There's no sound at first. The youngster in the film stuffs the glass bottle half-full of toilet paper, which he douses with alcohol that he smuggled outside.

Then the kid catches a live skink from a pocket canyon down the street. Once the killing jar is screwed shut, the fumes poison the lizard. After trembly pinched gasps, its breathing stops. The experiment proceeds. The youngster waits to be sure. The black glossy scales lose their rainbow sheen, the two yellow stripes ooze mucous. The mouth gapes.

The boy removes the small corpse from the killing jar and places it on a pine shingle. He slits open the pale belly with a razor blade and fingernail scissors. Parts the skin with eyebrow tweezers and pins the flaps to the wood with sewing needles. There is no blood. He bares the lungs, those pale balloons, and the viscera.

The dissection unfolds.

The boy's brothers and sister lean forward to look. He's the oldest and has taken charge of the autopsy.

"Oooh, it's breathing," they recoil.

Sure enough, the tiny pale sacs have come back from the dead. They expand and contract with each breath.

"Do something," the other children plead.

The BB-sized lungs fill and empty. The heart pumps. The splayed reptile claws the air and tries ro run, nailed on its back.

Bile rises in the boy's throat; the wriggling won't cease. What should he do? This mangled cemetery should have died in the fumes—why is he always screwing up when he tries to do things? *The boy's father mocks his "bear hands" that break objects that he tries to fix. His mother cries when he disappoints her, which is due.* The pale balloons that are the lungs catch the boy's panicked gaze. The scissors snip them in half.

Already, his siblings have fled.

Rage boils over because no one will help. They'll laugh and call him stupid. His stomach heaves at the experiment gone bad. That's when he lunges and chops off the lizard's head. Stabs with a pocketknife so hard that he gouges the wood. There's small blood this time.

Guzmán spits on the green campus lawn and massages his neck. That wasn't Juanito's movie he just watched. An imaginary phone rings somewhere, and Guzmán's picks up by habit. "Paging Dr. Freud, Dr. Sigmund Freud—please, dial the operator! A kid needs psychotherapy stat!"

There's a laugh if the message wasn't so obvious.

Would Rhoda have advised the young Frankenstein to stop the experiment? What would she do with the carcass? Silvio would taunt, "finish it, sissy! Bury the thing."

And at that moment, Molca decides to track down Lyle Carson, drop in on the acting vice president. Molca will pretend to offer his services so that he can find out who's sending thugs to waylay the parson. Let's play the turncoat spy and find out the bad guys.

Guzmán clambers to his feet, dusts himself off, and slings on the backpack.

He imagines Lyle's questions once he shows up: "Whose side are you on, Judas? Why backstab your friends?"

Why sell out? the flyweight reasons. *Good question. I'll reply just barely. Let Lyle fill in the blanks himself. Don't lie, Lyle's not dumb. Make him do the mental work.*

My answer: Who'd stay stuck at a shelter? Professor Carson. Especially a place that's on life support! The redevelopment committee marks a big red X. Progress comes first, right? That's America! Head West in a bulldozer! To own the future, make home expendable. Someone else's, at least

Get going, Molca thinks to himself. Enough mind games champ.

But the hot sun tugs at Guzmán's resolve. Is he pretending to switch over to the enemy, using a cover story about saving his own skin? Or is he actually selling out Pastor Quixote because Molca's lost his sweet Dulcinea, his Lady of Hope? Rhoda stands by Saint Steve of the Windmills, no matter what. If that's not love, what is it?

Molca stops. Just say that to Lyle! Just mention Rhoda. Lyle's not immune to jealousy either. Make her ex-husband forget that Molca's the one under the microscope. He's supposed to be for sale. This Siamese mind, a deer and a fox yoked together. *A mestizo, no less, named the grinding stone.*

Before braving the Amnesiology Building, Guzmán tosses his gum in the trash.

The stale air inside needs scrubbing. There's no security guard or central reception counter. Surveillance cameras are on. At the Office of Planned Giving, a mammoth class roster and Professor Carson's schedule of office hours are posted on the door. That's university policy.

Lyle's showing the other faculty that he can do it all, teach, administer, and serve the community. A professor who joins management rarely teaches. (The vice president's own book, by the way, is required class reading, five hundred copies.)

"Hello," Guzmán calls at the VP's threshold since no one's in sight.

"Professor Carson's away." A head peeks over a stack of mid-term exams like a sentry, "Office hours are canceled."

Guzmán points at the deskful of student bluebooks, "Another shift at the edu-factory."

"Oh, I'm his grader, factotum—a scrivener actually." The assistant's gaze is flat as his voice.

"'I'd prefer not to,'" Molca sneaks in a passage of literature, trying for a shock of recognition and a favor. "*Orale, profe,* I'm a student and a handyman at a homeless shelter downtown. Professor Carson heads the redevelopment committee.

"The Settlement, right? Blow your house down, huff and puff! The story's in the news," the graduate assistant is not the usual bureaucrat.

"The guy in charge is Pastor Bentham," Guzmán returns.

"Named for a philosopher, right?" the scrivener shows off his knowledge.

"Utility outfielder." Molca nods. "Tell your boss that the Chicano ex-boxer came by looking for work. "I'm Molca or Jósue Félix Guzmán, take your pick.

"Indeed," says the scrivener, "work for what?

"Ever slept at a shelter?" parries Guzmán.

"That close," the scrivener holds up a thumb and forefinger, while he checks around in case someone's listening. "I'm in graduate school care of the loan office. Progress is slow; the meter's running."

Molca laughs like a squeaky gate and aims a finger to his head. "I'm a third-year sophomore. Arrested sort of, but willing to learn. Tell you what, *profe*," Molca ventures, We've got a room in the basement ready for administrators."

Professor Carson's at a meeting," agrees his assistant.

"Exactly," Molca returns point-blank, "Any damage?"

"They're headed downtown, your way," advises the scrivener. "He and James Hannity from the Alliance of Churches. Furious. Seen the newspaper?" The teaching assistant reaches into a drawer and retrieves the local section.

Page one features a story about Rhoda's once-in-a lifetime find at the Settlement. Molca reads fast. Rare artifacts include prize baskets, hunting weapons, clothing made from fur and pelts. And Harrington's research notes bring back the dead, so detailed are the interviews with the last members of now extinct tribes. Plus, his unmailed personal letters to Carobeth read like a novel, according to the reporter.

The article closes with an announcement about the display's opening date, today in fact.

Molca hands back the edition, and the assistant returns it to a drawer. "Drats, here's a moth," says the man, slapping the air though there's nothing. "Turn off the light!" He signals a thumbs up. "This desk is information central, if you know where to search."

"Forget I was here, okay," Guzmán interrupts for Rhoda's sake because she's in enough trouble. Her plan to save the shelter might work, though. So might he have a chance with her? And Molca realizes, *she surprised you again!* Why hope? You hail from separate worlds. She's part Athena, part Venus. Maybe that's how to win her. Prove that you can shape-shift too. Whose face matches a driver's license ever, homeboy?

Guzmán puts on his sunglasses, squaring them on the bridge of his nose. Reality's constructed, Perception's a habit of mind, That's how she talks.

Rhoda, though, is not here to help with the ruse. "I guess I missed the vice president," Molca points at a clock above the door. "Thanks for the help, *profe*. Time to rally downtown."

"You're welcome," replies the scrivener, "Call me Bartleby." He pauses for a moment, as if there's something else. But then he swats at the air while disappearing behind the stack of bluebook exams.

As Molca leaves the office, someone's singing quietly, "I'd prefer not to be rescued."

21

THE MISSION STATEMENT of the Settlement's small museum, let it be clear, is to publicize the unburied artifacts from the dig as well as to champion the science of archeology. Now that the Harrington find is in the mix, how does Rhoda mount an exhibit? Especially given the do-or-die shelter politics. Although there's little time to prepare for visitors, the more public interest the better for winning support.

Aside from Harrington's unlabeled boxes of collected material, which include fieldnotes, journals, ritual objects, and implements from Native American daily life, there are his unmailed letters to Carobeth. Can archeology prove that he wrote them? In regard to protecting privacy, Harrington, Carobeth, and George Laird are deceased.

Rhoda will pursue the likely author using three sources. The unmailed pleas to Carobeth. The basket that holds the unsent letters. And Carobeth's biography of Harrington, *Encounter with an Angry God*, which mentions his attempt to call off their divorce. Passages from the book can be scaled up for viewers. Also, Rhoda will cross reference the unposted Carobeth letters with public records about their separation.

Who else would have made such a plea? And yet Harrington never opened his heart to anyone. (Which explains, perhaps, why the letters were never sent?) Rhoda has samples of Harrington's handwriting, which she can juxtapose with excerpts from the stillborn missives.

The basket-container holding the letters matches one on campus. Lab tests prove that both baskets are of Karuk design. And the one at the college is tagged in Harrington's script and names the weaver and when she gave him the piece.

Harrington's biography refers to San Diego many times. That's where Carobeth lived with her mother and father after they moved from Texas. Harrington taught college linguistics and anthropology at Balboa Park, which is close to downtown. Rhoda has early photographs of the city including the rundown hotel where Harrington might have lived, the rooming-house that morphed into the Settlement. The fact that his papers and records are at this location doesn't prove that Harrington left them behind. But the question is whether Harrington's the author.

She throws open the museum doors to check the size of the space as well as the light and ventilation. The exhibit will be as ready as time allows.

Outside there's shade and a garden view for any visitors.

She stands still for a moment as the sun descends and imagines her ex-husband's reaction to the Harrington project. *Zozobrar,* there's his expression of contempt, an old Spanish word that means, "To drown in a backwater hamlet, to suffocate in a hick town." The term is from colonial New Mexico, although modern Santa Fe is where Lyle was born. Lyle despises inferiors, all those beneath him. Lesser minds press their ears to your walls, all gossip. The echo kills you, the envy and resentment.

Maritime clouds scud over the buildings, and the wind-roiled shadows are chilly. Her sweater is back in the lab. This time of the day is when Lyle ambushed her and Steve by the gym, as the minister eyed him like a snake.

"*Those halfbreed genízaro castas*"—there's Lyle's epithet for low-class Indians with no place of their own. "Not worth a ditch of running water. Just like that mongrel *Molca.*"

She rubs her temples and recalls that Harrington and Carobeth don't like Chicanos either and consider them an adulterated race lacking a culture of their own.

Anyone at a shelter is no better than a deracinated Indian to her ex. Lyle nicknames Doc Manny *Saint Subsequent* or *Meister Aerosols*, a puff of smoke, a whiff of gas. Steve's moniker is Padre Remus, the white homeboy who farms a hill of beans! Po' folk is his calling.

Guzmán once teased her that, "The padre sports his crucifix; you worship Saint Darwin. What's up with you two, feeling superior to us gentiles?" Molca juked a little footwork as if he was still in the ring bobbing and weaving.

"Doubt is my fish," she returned like a shot. But she wondered, *who's stuck with old ways of thinking?*

Rhoda imagines how the boy must feel about his elders. Those poor old ghosts!

A ghost haunts one of the shelter's rooms, supposedly, maybe from when the place was a hotel. A woman in green satin, torn at the shoulder. A mulatta or dark Irish or *Mexicana*, perhaps? Is she a daughter of *Alta California,* or Colonial México, who surrendered her family's land after the Mexican American War? A captain's wife, perhaps, who jumped ship in San Diego? Maybe a working woman arrived from other parts?

When Rhoda was a girl, especially her teens, her mother tried to protect her from growing up too fast, even to the point of deciding on dates and a curfew. Thelma, though, considers herself a realist not a prude. A car's backseat isn't neutral territory.

When Rhoda told her mother about filing for a divorce, Thelma tiptoed around the weather and Rhoda's plans. After several moments, Rhoda coaxed, "Come on, Mom, I'm listening."

"What more could I have done?" Thelma wondered. "As smart as you are, Rhoda, with all your accomplishments?"

"Flattery, Mom?"

"That's not how I meant it, not like that," Thelma stammered and caressed her daughter's cheek. "You're my youngest."

"He's my mistake, Mom," Rhoda said. "Mine, no one else!"

"I should have insisted. Don't trust him," Thelma ventured. "A man who sorts his kin by blood, by race; what of his wife? She's a woman."

"We're German and Scotch-Irish, aren't we?" mused Rhoda. "Besides, times change, or so I thought. He's modern, well educated. Of my generation."

I put away caution for love, Rhoda realizes. Mom didn't. Progress isn't a rising line on a graph just because people drive cars. Once a chariot was modern. In Thelma's house in San Pedro, an old fireplace is boarded up behind a remodeled wall. There's an old superstition, *the Salamander haunts fire*. Does it matter that the counterfeit electric hearth sells on the shopping channel?

Rhoda walks to the shelter's main building and takes an elevator to the third floor, a refurbished dormitory for women. From this vantage point, she checks the street. A stone's throw below are two small annexes where families with children can shelter the night. The city would prefer stadium parking.

A broom closet nearby conceals a ceiling panel. Scuffmarks on the floor remind her that she and Juanito searched the attic for antiques, with flashlights and a ball of string.

She pulls the door shut and then takes the stairs down instead of the elevator.

On the ground floor, the computer room is busy, although the scent of stew and corn bread wafts from the kitchen.

Rhoda passes the rectory but doesn't knock.

22

MONSTERS OVERRUN AN island and then they are tamed. That story the boy Juanito recalls—though he wants not to think of bad things as he and Doc lounge by the garden. Padre Steve just waved from the chapel where he's preparing the evening service for the few who show up. One arm remains in a sling. The boy wonders, being a minister didn't save him from getting hurt. Juanito's church in Shelltown wants him to make his first communion. The priest says it's for his protection.

And Juanito recalls Steve's cut. The blood. Molca remains missing after they were attacked, no one knows where he is. Juanito ticks on his fingers the friends who are close by. Doc who's alseep in his chair. Rhoda in her lab. The padre.

The youngster imagines wide horns, wider than he is tall, the points sharp daggers—huge beasts that trample the fields of *taro* and sweet potatoes. The brutes were a gift to *King Kamehameha the First* from an English sea captain, only a few head. The Hawaiian king proclaimed a taboo on the cattle, a *kapu*, which outlawed hunting the beasts under pain of death.

Thus the monsters are protected by a king's edict and attack people on sight. The Big Island of Hawai'i isn't safe. Juanito closes his eyes, which doesn't shut off the images. Monsters gore local farmers in the fields, the gatherers of wood, the feather hunters. Native *kanakas*, called the "eyes of the land," bury their dead at night and repair what damage they can. Warriors won't take up their spears because of the *kapu*, and even the king's messengers are killed.

Juanito imagines his father's reaction, "Learn a lesson, you pussy. Learn how to fight."

The story goes that imported cowboys arrive in the Islands from California, Spanish-speaking horsemen who are called *paniolos* afterward, Mexican cowhands who round up the wild herds. These riders, called *vaqueros*, are hired by Polynesian royalty, the *ali'i*, who cross the Pacific to *Alta California*, observe the cowboys in action, and bring them back to Hawaii.

Some of these paniolo cowboys marry Hawaiian women and have mixed children who are called hapa. "One day I'll visit that place," Molca has told him. "Maybe they're cousins."

Rhoda and the youngster found that story from the Sandwich Islands in a dusty trunk, handwritten, in a sort of notebook like for school.

The scent of the sandalwood sticks in the boy's mind, and he's thankful. Juanito takes a breath and lets his mind wander elsewhere. Finding treasure he's good at. Squeezing through narrow places where he fits. The story about monster cattle is different. He falls off a cliff.

Which is why he prefers to be behind the walls, despite the spiders and the dark. Especially with Molca unaccounted for. The blind passageways, the narrow twists and turns, require a flashlight. But there's no monsters. Silence is welcome. The grown-ups go off by themselves when they need to. He has to wait. That absence is theirs. Behind the walls is for him.

The boy glances over at Doc again who is asleep in the garden chair. Should he wake him before it's dark?

Right now, there's silence. He can dream as he likes.

Rhoda taught Juanito how to do more than just rummage through attics and cellars for fun, but like archeologists doing science. They've recovered ancient picket signs from the old International Longshore and Warehouse Union days in the '30s. Even copies of "broadsides" about robber barons delivered from a "soapbox." Half those words confuse the boy.

Unexpected things is what Juanito prefers. A knotted rabbitskin blanket chewed by moths. Indian people made them. Sometimes the knots brand the tribe.

Pieces of cowhide cured and stiff, ready to manufacture leather. Cattle horns even, two to a pair. Moldy sea-otter pelts; and deer moccasins or elk probably, decorated with seashells, from when sailing ships roamed *Alta California*.

Pirates smuggled stuff under the noses of the Mexican custom authorities. That entry's on the Internet.

And in a boarded-up closet, he and Rhoda found that traveling story about bighorn cattle killing people, in a sandalwood trunk crammed with a woman's belongings and a Bible. Once the shelter had been a hotel.

The Stingaree, an old sailors' district, once fronted these premises. Ministers stormed into the redlight district preaching against whiskey and sin.

Today there are guided tours retracing the saloons and flophouses, which were a magnet for drinking and whores. The boy's seen stuff happening in back alleys today that he won't tell the parish priest and the nuns. They'd insist even more on catechism.

The monster story comes with another fact that he can't mention.

The overseer for the Hawaiian king *Kamehameha III*, the overseer who hired the *vaqueros* or cowboys, carried the title of *konohiki*. As a royal steward appointed by the Hawaiian monarch he dined with the highest society in *Alta California*, which was México then in the 1830s. In San Diego, says the story, he met with Roman Catholic prelates; government officials including the *alcalde*, or mayor; and business leaders; plus the heads of the most well-connected families.

So special was the *konohiki's* visit that a state dinner was celebrated in his honor.

The evening of the sumptuous feast amid the pomp and ceremony, one of the bishop's assistants, who enjoyed wine too much, demanded of the overseer if his people had killed and eaten Captain Cook, the famous English explorer who was ambushed and slain by Polynesian warriors on the Big Island of *Hawai'i*. Cook's body disappeared after the attack.

The bishop's assistant with the dogged mind had migrated from colonial New México where his family had helped prosecute the witchhunts in the beseiged outpost of *Abiquiú*. The inquisition there arrested local Indians for devil worship, displaced *genízaro* slaves from outlaw tribes in that region. California, though, was different, and had a chain of missions founded by Junipero Serra situated along El Camino Real, the King's Road. Local indians were Christianized. But in the mind of the assistant prelate from New México, all natives are devil worshippers. Neither the Church nor intermarriage purifies bad blood.

The *konohiki*, however, was a native Hawaiian who had been educated by missionaries in the Islands and mentored there by the Spaniard Don Francisco de Paula Marin, *King Kamehameha the Great's* advisor. Thus the *konohiki* had parleyed with Russian sea captains hungry for glory, British lords extending the Empire, and American traders coveting the land.

Given the *konohiki's* bona fides, he deflected the bishop's assistant's inquiry about cannibalism by toasting the Spaniard Don Marin who brought the pineapple to *Hawaii*. This gift transformed the Islands into plantations, although once these outposts were separate kingdoms unknown to the West. Thousands died after contact.

The Catholic priest ignored the *konohiki's* salute to Don Marin, a double-edged riposte about progress, and repeated his query about whether Hawaiians feasted on Captain Cook. None of the local San Diego officials thought to intervene—not the mayor, not the bishop, not the fortress commandant. Diplomacy was ignored.

The *konohiki* frowned and stood up to leave, yet thanked his hosts for their hospitality. The bishop's assistant, though, persisted. Had the Hawaiians devoured the English explorer?

Do Christians eat the body of their god and drink his blood? the *konohiki* asked the priest. "Holy Communion, the feast is called."

The banquet's orchestra saved the moment, A flourish of music keyed the *konohiki's* departure.

Who gave the order to play? Juanito wonders. He guesses a physician or a teacher.

Juanito's heard the Church mass celebrate the exact words "body and blood." The youngster's listened to the offertory, and read the missal. But the boy won't ask just anyone about why the white wafer or the chalice with wine made people so angry in the story. He lives in the barrio where the Church is strong. Certainly, he won't ask about Captain Cook in Sunday school. That would cost a confession and a rosary.

Even when Juanito asks Doc to explain the story, Manny turns to Rhoda, "You're the teacher, okay. Unpack the meaning so he understands. On the Eighth Day, Man invented Propaganda. That's the best I can do."

All Rhoda answers is, "Please Juanito, sometimes we have to trust silence. Go play outside!"

Juanito understands that words cause trouble. Cuss words, dirty words. The *konohiki* story is like that, although he's not sure exactly. Friends, though, share secrets and keep them no matter what. So he'll wait for later.

Near the fountain cofferdam across from Doc; the boy studies garden spiders while he minds the sheer pit. Close by the edge, wasps hide their nests in the dirt. And right by the bougainvillea bush, while he was hunting bugs, is where he once overheard Rhoda and Doc Manny talking about Molca and him. They were wondering out loud, talking science— but talking about him.

These are their words. *Why is it that when Guzmán goes missing, so does Juanito? The two of them are like paired quantum particles, two mirrored bits of matter that are in phase somehow. What happens to one affects the other, no matter the distance between them. They're entangled.*

Juanito fathoms that Molca and he are like twins. Molca said that they're doubles or *cuates*. *So Molca has to be close, right here where I am,* the boy assumes. *And since Doc's with me, he has to come back.*

Trust has to act. It's a promise.

23

LYLE'S DEPARTMENT CHAIR, Ernie Spiller, just recommended Lyle for a terminal year at the university, despite the fact that the department committee representing Lyle's colleagues voted for awarding Lyle tenure and promotion to associate professor. At this stage of Assistant Professor Lyle Carson's review, the tally for his advancement is even: one vote for and one against. Next, the candidate's application will be weighed by his college, the dean's yes or no included. And Lyle's position as acting vice president in the Office of Planned Giving matters to the college's fund-raising, which should give him a boost. Trouble is that Provost Marcie Tarpon wants all donations and bequests to go through her office, not the department chairs or the college deans, which doesn't make friends. And Provost Tarpon is Lyle's boss.

Chair Spiller wants to fire Lyle—and not just because Spiller dismisses Lyle's research on seafaring canoes as irrelevant speculation. How then did African people settle South America before Asian people migrated there from Siberia? In Tierra del Fuego, at the isolated tip of Chile, DNA confirms the genetic link to Africa although Spiller won't hear it.

"If seafaring signifies progress, then why aren't we kinder to each other?" That's Rhoda he's hearing, offering a comment after Lyle's open lecture last week, which he presented to his peers. Her banter sticks like a migraine. "Kindness" indeed. Is that why she removed herself from casting a vote, recused herself from any decision although they're not married anymore.

Retribution's come calling, my ex-to-be twice, my dearest Rhoda. I told you, don't get in my way. Lyle Carson checks his wristwatch. He just caught a glimpse of his former wife at a third-story window. Payback comes steep. She had the chance to help him and didn't.

Lyle shakes his head at Rhoda's notion that symbols define culture and key behavior. According to her, archeology confirms that human sacrifice is the oldest form of mathematics. Blood is a gift to the gods, an exchange of a life for their protection. The "archogenics" hypothesis, her pet project, features how people represent the world, then and now. The point is that people construct reality in the same old way. Lyle grinds his teeth, why should such unmoored speculation merit the rank of full professor?

A stake through the heart, sweet Lily, meant just for you, but by way of Dr. Reese. Lyle sniggers at the pathetic physician and retired medical officer dozing by the knoll. Our invalid cures people by testifying in court, voicing his opinions. Dr. Reese molds like old cheese while the stadium construction is stuck on hold a few blocks away.

Meanwhile, no one cares that Lyle's a scholar. His intellect doesn't count. Lyle's career depends on building a sports park—genuflecting to money in that dusty cathedral. The situation is absurd, comic, good for laughs. When did the university become a sports channel?

From beneath the shaded bougainvillea, Lyle takes a bead on some of the shelter residents shuffling past. "Bums and losers," Lyle mutters, which hits close to home. What about a college professor spying on a damn old physican who opposes a stadium? The Settlement's greenery spills out of concrete as if spray painted. Toil in the weeds Lyle must.

Sad stories come three for a quarter, spare change anyone?

Zozobra! Lyle mouths the Spanish word from New Mexico signifying death by a thousand cuts. He's no better than a peon weeding tomato vines, bent over in the brain. Ordinary people live just so—scraping off shit same day after day. That's life in this village. Be grateful that the air's fresh, at least. Meanwhile, *zozobra* taunts him—boredom that kills. How mediocre is death. Even a fool passes the final exam.

However, a bailiff's on the way right now to deliver an injunction to the good doctor, a cease and desist order that won't let him testify in court. Good riddance old geezer, Lyle thinks. *A man is master of his own isolation—that's all there is finally!* An informant notified Homeland Security about Dr. Reese. According to the Patriot Act, the retired commander wrongfully possesses classified military research, including patients' medical records. So the ancient mariner's testimony in court has been suppressed—the litigation against the government can't proceed.

So much for martyrs! As for you, my dear Rhoda, let that fountain serve as your epitaph, that unmounted hole in the earth.

Someone's been busy, indeed, in this theatre of the absurd. Merit should carry the day, not politics. But everything's for sale in this country, ideas included.

A den of big egos counting publications, that's Beehive U. How hard they work at cloning themselves, these academicians. A buzzard should be their mascot, this army of hermaphrodites humping each other. A keyhole is their universe. They can spell but not dream. Compute but not paradigm shift.

Conceptual illiterates are deciding his future, for all their titles and diplomas.

Provost Tarpon's imprimatur, by the way, is the vote that counts for promotion, not the chair, not the faculty committee, not even the dean of the college. Her decison only decides who's tenured. And Lyle reports directly to her. His vice-president's office is four doors down the hall.

Lyle's scholarship, his version of peopling the ancient world, includes the likelihood of prehistoric boats crossing the Pacific. Braving rough water is old as making fire. But wood hulls and fiber rope and woven rigging rot and leave no trace. So nothing can be retrieved for carbon dating. The proof of sea travel is circumstantial. Consider how the ancient temple of *taputapuatea* was the spiritual hub of farflung Polynesia long before Europe built cathedrals. Sailing canoes, double-hulled *waka*, returned to the altar at *Ra'iatea* to pay homage from crossings to Chile and Santa Barbara even. They navigated by the sun and the stars and the ocean currents. And these transpacific marathons occurred long before Columbus. How many generations perfected the craft?

Why assume only Polynesians put out to sea? Why not people from Africa ten thousand years in the past?

And back at the Settlement, Professor Lyle Carson eyes a dry fountain beside a hole in the ground. What a waste: all the money, all that effort. Just like that sports complex, a gilt playground.

Today at the college before Lyle came downtown, his stadium committee met in emergency session. They will offer Pastor Bentham full market value for the shelter property in order to move the stadium forward. A money manager, of course, set the price and interest rates. The deal to vacate the site includes a relocation bonus, if the mission signs the contract in the next twenty-four hours.

James Hannity from the Alliance of Churches informed the committee about Dr. Reese's setback in court, the injunction that silences him from testifying about secret research.

Reverend Hannity gestured at the manicured hedges on campus, speaking in a slow measured voice as if from a pulpit. "Good stewards keep out the weeds."

"We couldn't force Pastor Bentham's resignation, James," Lyle parried. "You tried an expensive ad campaign, and it tanked."

Hannity flushed deep as his tie. He hates first names.

"There are no other women, no scandals," Lyle patted the Reverend's shoulder. "Bentham's finances are clean. What sort of person lives on fifteen dollars a day?"

"The sidewalk minister, our Knight of the Ordinary," Hannity sneered. "No car, no savings or investments—our holy man lives out of a suitcase. For entertainment he plants vegetables. Pastor Bentham pays himself fifteen hundred a month in wages. He turns around and sends Regina a thousand in alimony leaving five-hundred clear. Five-hundred American dollars a month. That's what he lives on. Feels guilty, betcha, which explains the blood money!"

"That's why we nuke him," Lyle goaded. "His precious mission. First, the bailiff serves the good doctor that injunction. In the meantime, you serve our swarthy ex-champion that subpoena that orders him to appear before the labor board!" Guzmán supervises the cleaning crews and needs to explain why a charity runs a janitorial business.

"Saint Steve the Daft," scoffed brother James. "Pays the resident's in cash. Who does that?"

Which reminded Lyle that the real target is the parson, not the halfbreed, not the leech.

Lyle let Hannity rant for a moment in front of the committee so that he gins up his courage.

"The comic convention brings out the freaks, James," Lyle interrupted. "Give our barrio boy a welcome, sir."

"The 12th and C station," Hannity shot back. "*Bienvenidos* to the *peon*!"

Bring a bodyguard Mr. Hannity or lose some teeth, Lyle hopes, as Lyle waits at the shelter on a decrepit old man. Get in Molca's face, Your Worship. In public no less. When our favorite spic lays you out, oh the jubilation!

No matter what happens, Lyle can't lose. Let the earth devour them all!

Except right now, Lyle's digging weeds at the shelter, chopping cotton. Bent over in the brain spying on Dr. Manfred Saul Reese, as the bouganvillea sloughs its skin. What's the cure for *zozobra*, death by boredom? And that question brings up another thought. Why does the Zuni tribe have a fetish representation for every animal, except one?

"Why is there no fetish for the vulture?" Lyle asked a tribal elder once, during a college internship in the field, and Lyle pointed at a soaring speck in the sky. *Zopilotes* are desert sentries, eyes in the air.

"The vulture lives on death," the old geezer gestured up with a balled fist and a thumb. "We do not speak of it." The nightwatch tossed a pinch of earth and dusted his palms. And yet a carving of a bear signifies strength, the butterfly represents transformation. So why no buzzard?

Time runs out; there's the shadow. It circles overhead. And death's cousin decides promotion at a college.

Outside the mission compound at that very moment, the Reverend Stephen Bentham calls out for the *coyote* brat, "Juanito, Jua-ni-to . . ." Our beloved parson must be babysitting.

Youngsters role the dice when it comes to parents. Might the right guidance better a kid's chances in life, even one individual? Break the spiral that sinks a person, Figure the odds of such a reversal happening. Juanito could be a physician like Commander Reese, maybe a professor like Rhoda. Or a serial killer with a boxing fetish.

"Come out, you autistic little shit," Lyle mutters from his leafy cover. Come out, come out, Asperger's child! Come watch the bailiff smack down your coach! Someday soon, Padre Esteban himself will be sued for sheltering illegal aliens. That's you beaming boy, yes, Rhoda's muddy promise from a new generation? Where were you born?

Win or lose, the water turns off.

As for Saint Lily of Bart, our mother inferior, Lyle just caught a glimpse of his ex-wife at a window, phone to her ear. He eyes the three-story drop.

Yet as Lyle waits for the bailiff to serve the court order to Dr. Reese, Rhoda's archeology trenches nearby remind him that John Peabody Harrington was ahead of his time. Whole tribes were going extinct in his day, so the man transcribes their languages and customs while camping out of his battered Model T—a cloistered scribe subsisting on sour mush and cheap stew. The university crowd mocked him, the so-called experts in his field.

What shames Harrington, though, is his divorce. Running after Carobeth, trying to reconcile with her, leaves him pathetic and small like everybody else. Fear not courage informs Harrington's solitude, the fear of death. Otherwise Carobeth has no power to make him her fool.

24

THERE BY THE garden in his favorite chair, hat on his knee, Doc Manny warms in the sun as his life replays and resets. Memory unfurls like a sail beating upwind, such is its reach.

His father, a disabled veteran who survived the sinking of the cruiser Indianapolis, had wanted to graduate from medical school and then attend officer's college. "Do what I couldn't," his father charged his oldest son. "Break the hex, and be somebody!" When the Indianapolis went down, his father lost a leg to the sharks, not his dream.

Manny threw back his shoulders whenever he left the house. His family's eyes were on him.

Since seventeen, when Manny was captain of his high-school academic team, he's sought distinction to stand out by merit. In college, Manny competed in boxing and chess. He joined the International Club, which included members from Sweden and Hong Kong and Egypt. Like his dad, he wanted to travel. Bridging worlds, whether in sports or with people, became an emblem for striving. He tried dating, but women were better as friends. As long as he stayed busy, he managed to fit in.

He won a Naval Reserve Officer's Training Corps scholarship, graduated from college, and then earned an officer's commission. By then, however, the Vietnam War threatened to call up the draft. His dad insisted, "not my son. This isn't our war." Manny applied for medical school and was accepted right off in the Ivy League. The navy covered his expenses as he specialized in internal medicine. He was the best diagnostician in his class. Upon graduation, his first military assignment was aboard a navy hospital ship where he was promoted to lieutenant and offered an appointment in the regular navy.

Aboard a medical vessel cruising off the coast of Danang, the horizon opens from every quarter, despite the influx of combat casualties. Line of sight has no measure. The sky's incandescent; the night a star compass. The bow's wake blooms in the dark.

At the shelter this moment, however, Doc wishes there was time to help Juanito claim a future. There's a lot to make right. But Doc's ship is hard aground and sinking. Without hope, a new beginning isn't possible. And Doc weighs his military career, his double life when he lived in the shadows. Let secrets rule your decisions and existence becomes mere pantomime.

One voyage stands out.

Lieutenant Commander Reese is assigned to a helicopter platform ship, an LPH that's on a secret mission. As the vessel is at station-keeping off the Big Island of Hawaii, a lone H-3 Sea King swoops aboard with three civilian casualties all in grave condition from exposure to nerve agents.

The classified mission has unraveled. The remote tests in the island jungles were not far enough away from people. Hunters trek to the remote kipuka where the tests were conducted, and a Kona wind caught three of them in the open. A spotter aircraft broke radio silence and called in a medevac chopper that delivers the patients aboard ship.

On the amphibious carrier, crews in decontamination suits leap into action, strip the patients' clothes and hose down seawater. This is no drill. Brine sloshes underfoot as the litters are rushed to sickbay below deck where Dr. Reese is the medical officer in charge. The executive officer, or XO, the second-in command of the ship, lags behind the three civilian casualties, pressing a gas mask to his face.

"Hold fast, Dr. Reese. Don't begin treatment," the XO orders. "The captain's contacting headquarters."

Instead of suspending triage as ordered, Lieutenant Commander Reese injects the patients with atropine and diazepam to save their lives. The big *kanaka* hunter is slipping away *(Doc remembers his name, Ho'alu Pakua, Slack the Rope)*. A venous cutdown is imperative for shock and to prevent kidney damage.

"Hold fast, corpsman," the XO warns the doctor's enlisted assistant. But an underling's not the target.

The decon crew in blister suits, full hazardous material protection, step back and watch. Dr. Reese, who wears a caduceus, has medical authority aboard the vessel. The exec, a line officer, commands the bridge.

"Maintain the treatment I ordered, corpsman," Dr. Reese commands. "These patients are shedding the agent. Feel your lungs?"

The exec glares, but then coughs and clears out of the sickbay. The crew in space suits don't snap to attention as they do for the doctor. That insubordination goes down in the exec's blackbook, with all the other infractions against the Uniform Code of Military Justice.

After he's gone, the doctor warns the decon crew not to invite trouble. The leash is short for a court martial charging insubordination. He returns the men to duty.

Meanwhile, the patients' vital signs gallop and slow, crash and rebound. Under his breath the doctor's enlisted assistant remarks, "They'll call this an accident, sir, invent some story about volcanic fumes poisoning civilians."

"As you were, Doc," Lieutenant Commander Reese cautions the hospital corpsman. "The exec's on the warpath. I'm administering pralidoxime to keep them alive."

"The navy will strip your commission," the veteran petty officer coughs up froth. "They'll cover this up as if it never happened." He self-injects an ampule of atropine.

One of the patients, the red-haired islander, struggles to breathe and turns cyanotic. Dr. Reese inserts a breathing tube and debates a tracheostomy. He picks up a scalpel and makes an incision at the throat. With a ventilator installed that administers oxygen, he doublechecks the other patients.

The breathing machine trips on and off for an hour or so. Then the patient resumes respirations on his own, and it's disconnected. Are his lungs scarred, the poor bastard? Dr. Reese is adrift. What persists is the strangeness, as if staring through smoke.

Eight bells on mid-watch, the three gassed hunters are airlifted to Tripler Army Hospital under radio silence. After the medical helicopter clears the flight deck, a clean sweep with soapy water is ordered fore and aft. A curtain of salt water sprays the ship. No one confirms what just happened.

Dr. Reese submits a written request for clinical follow-ups of anyone exposed to the chemical agent—all affected personnel, including civilians. The government ordered the tests. Now follow through with the best medicine and standard of care.

A short while later, the executive officer pulled him aside and advised that venting gases from Kilauea Volcano disabled the hunters.

"My request for medical intervention stands, sir, with due respect."

"Your opinion, Dr. Reese, isn't the navy. An official statement was just released. Be advised, and man your post!"

A military physician swears two oaths: to patients and to country. National security had trumped Hippocrates. When the doctor's amphibious aircraft carrier docked at Pearl Harbor, however, Dr. Reese hand-delivered his report to the fleet commander, bypassing the chain of command.

When he returned to his vessel, he packed his belonging, his pictures from home last of all. He took a navy shower, which saved water. Afterward, wrapped in a towel, he unpacked a clean uniform and attached his collar insignias of rank and specialty.

And he thought to himself, "To act as an officer" or "To swear a physician's oath"—you're stuck shipmate. *Since you enlisted, you've led a double life.* To do or to be are phantom choices. Now you're erased, trapped between verbs.

A week after he notified headquarters about the casualties, the collateral damage, Lieutenant Commander Reese is reassigned from the amphibious carrier to remote Kwajalein Island as a medical officer. There's only an hour to disembark from the carrier. The military flight transits through Guam, and at Kwajalein, there's only a landing strip not an airport. Mail takes weeks to arrive, and it's censored. Kwajalein monitors distant atolls for nuclear tests and worst.

Back at the Settlement in his chair by the garden, Manny's stretches his numb left arm. *I was transferred to Kwajalein, right, not Fanning Atoll. Fanning is in the Line Island, and that was a distress call, an emergency evacuation.* Doc Manny straightens his elbow as if pointing a course.

Nitroglycerine tabs for his heart are in a vest pocket. The coastal air settles in his chest.

Seated across from the still fountain with his eyes closed and the famous hat on his lap, Doc Manny notices Rhoda standing at a high window while talking on her phone. Has her mother Thelma taken a turn for the worse?

And Doc concludes that Thelma's doing as well as she can, thanks to Rhoda.

As for him, once you hide who you are, there's a lot to put right. Redemption only works if you live long enough.

And he wonders, *Why live in shadows so as not to offend, don a mask? For honor, because you're afraid? What sort of person lives underground, divided from himself? There's a poem about lovers who can never be one. "As lines so Loves oblique may well/ Themselves in every angle greet:/ But ours so truly parallel,/ Though infinite can never meet."* Doc imagines an asymptote, merging lines that never quite cross. Aren't Rhoda and the minister a near miss like that because he trusts God, and she trusts a microscope?

What about Doc himself—split through the soul, living by proxy so as not to offend. Woe to the righteous, no matter which chapter and verse. Conformity has a frail half life. When do commandments solve passion or bridge the head and the heart?

And for an instant, beyond the unmet fountain, just there by the furrows, Juanito turns fresh compost into the soil with a spading fork. The warmth glistens on his brow, sun sculpted.

Doc points to the apparition and rubs his chest. The four of them put in a garden.

White grubs and pale crickets boil out of the replenished moist earth. A wrentit darts in to feed on pillbugs. A scrub jay, an interloper from the chaparral, gorges on leftover seeds and melon rinds, oblivious to the noise from traffic. Drawn by the flurry of plumage, wild Amazon parrots zoom overhead. The bright air tastes feral.

Molca rolls up with another wheelbarrow of amendment as if conjured by a lamp. To help unload the compost, the boy too takes off his shirt. Agility and endurance, effortless and perfect, such is youth. Age can only marvel.

Why respect this old relic's passing, any of them.

And Manny breathes deep as the sun bends west. This soldier became a caretaker of codes, a guardian of stealth. Rhoda and Steve would never deny who they are. But for them, there's no middle ground

As for Doc, this seafarer requires an epitaph. Summer is past.

25

"DR. REESE," THE court messenger clears his throat, "Lieutenant Commander Manfred Saul Reese."

The old man struggles awake in his chair by the fountain.

"Dr. Reese, I have a judge's order!"

"What took you so long," Doc murmurs, "sure." He recognizes the court official. "The judge threw out my case, right," Doc pretends to toss a file.

"You can't testify in court, Dr. Reese—you're enjoined from speaking in public by the Secrets Act.

"Sealed the record like it never happened. No one's responsible."

"We're civilians now," the bailiff cuts him off, "not soldiers. Forget Iraq! The campaign of shock and awe never happened!"

"That cough of yours, from the war, right," answers Doc Manny. "Can't shake it?"

"They gave us a medal," snaps the official, who raps his chest.

"Sweep us under a field of crosses," murmurs the old man. "Sound taps. The oil fires rained soot! Who knows what else? We ran out of gas masks."

"Leave it alone," mutters the bailiff, as Juanito runs up from behind the squash plants. "Stand clear, sonny," the messenger snaps. "Don't be a sea lawyer." The crier spins on his heel and leaves.

"Why's he so mad?" asks Juanito

"He was a soldier," Manny answers.

"So were you."

"Yes. Because of me he remembers the past."

"Why do that?" the kid asks.

"I wonder," Doc Manny says, "I wonder? He chews on a pain pill and tries to swallow. Across the bay is a national cemetery.

"Do you need water?" asks the boy.

26

FROM A THIRD-STORY window, Rhoda's keeping an eye on Juanito who disappeared for a moment. She can't answer her phone right then. Once she spots him, she checks the message.

"Guzmán calling, Professora Bart. Answer, please! If you're at the shelter, protect Doc Manny. The judge just dismissed his case. A gag order is coming. Advise the padre.

"And watch yourself," Guzmán speaks over the static. "Your ex . . ."

Trolley noise clatters in the background. A tamale vendor offers, "three for ten dollars, *pollo* or *res*."

"I'm at 12th and C station," Guzmán confirms. "Hannity's waiting. Here he comes . . ."

"I'll tell Steve," hurries Rhoda, but the call drops. Moving closer to the window, she redials—with no luck.

Just then on the knoll, shelter security points a court messenger over to Doc Manny's chair.

The bailiff coughs into his sleeve, crosses over the grass, and raps the aluminum frame with an envelope. He's been to the shelter a few times.

Juanito runs to his friend.

Rhoda rushes downstairs

"He needs to wake up," offers the boy.

"Juanito, Juanito," Steve calls from the toolshed, as he searches for the youngster who he assumes is hiding.

Juanito grips the old man's wrists so he won't fall. The bones are thin, narrow as his own. "Doc Manny," he whispers, "Doc Manny, wake up!"

Across from the fountain, Lyle Carson slips away and heads for the exit. At least, Rhoda believes it's him. She dials emergency and calls to Steve.

"I just saw Lyle," pastor Bentham jogs over.

"Molca's at the 12th and C station," Rhoda hurries. "Hannity's waiting."

"Lyle must be headed there," the parson guesses, "to pile on."

"Can you manage?" Steve turns to pursue him.

Rhoda nods.

"I have to go," the padre tells the boy. "Take care of Doc, you and Rhoda." Bentham bends close to the old man. "Help's coming, Manny!"

Rhoda checks up and down for the medics. Residents yap by the curb, staring, gawking.

Juanito won't let go of Doc's hand. He gave his word: trust has to stay. But once Doc's safe, then maybe he can help Molca and Steve at the trolley.

Shadows lengthen as Doc Manny slumps in the chair. The boy wishes water was close. The fountain's not mounted yet and has to be set on the plinth.

Superman is pretend and can't budge the weight!

All around, twilight settles. Everything's going to pieces—that's how it seems. Pockets of darkness scatter the birds.

By the bouganvillea, just a minute ago, the boy saw Lyle Carson slink low like a stray cat. The ghosty old owl nailed to the roof sees all but can't speak. That's how the boy feels, up high but mute.

Rhoda and the boy lay Manny on the ground, while the spectators shout advice. She loosens his collar, Juanito the belt.

Juanito can't feel a pulse. He closes his eyes hard and imagines Doc telling a story as if he's all right.

"Once a ship of mine surveyed an atoll in the middle of nowhere, Fanning Island, nine hundred miles from Pearl Harbor. Took baseline measurements of thorium and cobalt in the fish and coconuts. Eniwitok's not that far by wind."

"Thorium and cobalt," whispers the boy who recognizes radioactive stuff.

Sometimes Doc talks like he's dreaming and assumes a kid can't follow.

"We evacuated a seaweed farmer with a gangrenous leg," the old man continues. "He cut himself offshore on the planting wire, and the wound festered. That smell sticks with me."

Now some folk at the shelter carry an odor from the streets. Once they check in, the first stop is to bathe. Juanito helps bundle the towels. The people outside must pretend not to notice, or wouldn't they give money for soap?

Doc Manny leans back in his chair and recalls the seaweed farmer at Fanning Island who was out of his mind. He sang a Kiribati song about "talkie talkie me." At least that's Doc's impression of the language since there was no one to translate.

"Should we call the medics again?" the boy breaks the trance.

Rhoda uses her sweater for a pillow, and searches up and down the street.

"Our ship was bound for Fanning Island, Tabuaeran, the local folk call it." Doc Manny's lost in time. "Cramped coral atoll, mid Pacific, a lost port of call. The steamships abandoned the place. Beautiful in its way. A culture of dancing. There's no physician, no electricity, no running water. Fanning is where we evacuated the patient, took him aboard our vessel. We tried hard as we could."

The old man stretches out an arm as if something's coming. Juanito chants, "wake up."

"Take this key to Rhoda's room," Doc Manny clasps his own left shoulder. "Fetch my briefcase. Bring it to me. Try to be quick. I'm very tired."

By the time Juanito returns with the bag, the Doc's lips are blue and his hands are cold. He won't let the boy call for help. Better to wait he says—Molca's on the way here. Juanito gives him his briefcase, and Doc Manny retrieves an envelope. "This is my will," the old man confirms.

"No," the boy recoils, "Take it back."

"I want you attend school away from here, Oakwood Academy—my alma mater. You're young," Doc Manny murmurs.

"I can't take back time," the old man tells him, and brings both fists to his chest.

The boy wipes his eyes because Doc hasn't moved on the ground.

"You've visited the campus with Molca and me. It's your decision to enroll. Your sister Serafina is on board if you do, and your mom. They're your guardians now. Your dad's back in jail.

"And there's money in the trust for Molca too," the old man continues. "Money for college so he can study full time. I've saved and invested for the hard years. There's some left. He'd make a good doctor, don't you think?"

"What about the padre?" the boy sighs. "What about the residents?"

"We trained the staff to help manage the place," answers Doc Manny. "Don't fret. They're good people. And there's Rhoda. Why don't you go find her."

"I won't leave," Juanito insists.

"Let me rest here by the garden." Doc Manny taps Juanito's arm. "I'll be okay. 'Slide and glide . . . ,'" he murmurs and loses his hat.

Rhoda kneels by Doc's side and starts CPR. Juanito checks his breathing again.

Now sometimes a falling egg from a nest spatters the ground or yolks the sidewalk. And nestlings are maimed by rats who sneak into broods and chew off a foot. The pink stub jerks in the air like a worm. The boy shies away from the sight.

Juanito imagines his father laughing at sissies.

"Fear is natural," Rhoda has told Juanito. "Something lets go when the lights turn off."

Juanito's seen an overdosed woman collapsed in a hallway. A heart attack victim turned up dead in his bunk.

"Wait here by the door," Doc told him. Juanito stepped back without thinking.

When E Flat trashed the garden and fell into the caisson for the fountain, the boy stared at the bloody concrete box. He knew better than to run in the dark, especially with archeology trenches nearby. E Flat wasn't just scared of getting caught. Something else chased him.

When the boy asked about E Flat, Rhoda said he scared himself. Who he's become.

"But E Flat's grown up. He's not a kid!" the boy marveled

"He feels buried," she answered.

By the time the ambulance arrives for Doc Reese, a chill smothers the boy. *Am I dead too?* he wonders. *Is this a sense of an ending?*

"Step back, folk!" exhort the medics. "Let us work."

Juanito grips Doc Manny's hand.

"Go help Molca and Steve!" Rhoda insists and tries to hug the boy. "I'll ride in the ambulance! Go to the station right now! Bring Steve and Molca back." She won't let him watch the resuscitation team.

Juanito brushes Doc's hat and hands her the fedora. She hangs it on the lawn chair and repeats, "please go." But the boy's thoughts are stuck. *Molca and Steve just traded punches when Doc wasn't there in the gym. Doc explained the commotion, the "three-ring circus" between Steve and Rhoda and Molca.*

And he wants to tell Rhoda that Doc's soul will fly away from all the ruckus. Manny's worn out. There's the boxing team to manage. The case in court. *And Steve loves Rhoda, maybe. And she loves him. Lyle Carson's stuck in the middle. Or is it Molca?*

Words are pantomime. Secrets own them. Without Doc Manny what happens to us? The good forgets how to act.

Doc has to get better, the boy thinks. So tell him that a cactus wren built a nest in the cholla. That his chair is waiting to watch the chicks.

The boy can't hear the birds as he rushes away to the trolley.

27

RIGHT BY THE shelter, just leaving the exit, a shadow saunters away to the commuter trolley station. "Don't worry, James," Professor Lyle Carson smirks to his cell. "I'll come handle Molca, since you two grown men can't. The cavalry's just minutes away." Lyle snaps shut the cover and strolls to the green-line tracks. All this trouble with a halfbreed dwarf *casta*. But it's all for the good. Let Hannity try the midget and hand him that subpoena. The dwarf will stub king James to size.

Juanito, meanwhile, runs to the station, although Doc's taken sick at the shelter. He hears a siren in the distance.

The stadium route is quickest, five blocks only. The boy sprints flat out. Beside the bare concrete struts for the stadium walls, a shovel-tusked Gomphotherium rests on the dirt. All the construction machines are shut down. There's no traffic because the streets are closed. Plumes of gasoline have to be fixed, plumes that leak underground.

Barricades block J Street, which leaves him the road.

Months back, the boxing team used to jog past the construction site early in the morning before school, when trucks were still lining up to haul away fill. Before digging resumed each day, archeologists inspected the trenches checking for fossils. Ancient whales swim in sandstone. Ammonites spiral through rock.

Juanito catches his breath across from the scraped pits for underground parking, and he walks past the piles of gouged earth that are bulldozed aside for ticket seats. Over the rubble, a shut-off Brachiosaurus stretches its neck. And the boy inhales deep and wonders, Are my eyes only live to dead bones? This place is for sports. Why be sad?

Last night, he streamed a nature program on the computer when he couldn't sleep. The narrator said that the entire earth's remade over and over. Old boulders melt in volcanoes, and lava spews up. Seas rise and fall burying trilobites in mud, and then the earth heaves up into mountains. Deserts are created, which bloom and then dry out from boom to bust.

And Juanito closed his eyes in bed and dreamed. Once this city was seafloor.

The trolley is a stage coach.

The shelter, a hotel.

Cities rise and fall and rise again, recycled by time. Rhoda shows him pictures of the Maya pyramids and the Colosseum, which were rebuilt over and over. Invaders and earthquakes leveled the walls. The survivors who put new floors on rubble were modern as us, building on wreckage. The good gets covered up. People start from scratch. And not everyone's kind.

Juanito takes off running again for the trolley station, flies by the ruins that guide him, squeezing by fences and dumpsters. Sometimes these city blocks transform in a day because of the construction. Cranes and trucks and bulldozers demolish the area so quick that he has to count streets to keep up. The map's in his head, though, all of a piece, his notebook, his portable tablet, his LED screen. He finds his way despite the dust and the chaos.

Molca tells a joke about the shelter downtown. Every day's shovel ready, under construction. "Some folk be low to the ground, like us."

Finally, Juanito arrives at the traffic barriers near the commuter line. Vehicles crawl past the tracks; People walk up from all sides. Trolley dancers on a makeshift stage twirl like planets for the tourists. Juanito dodges past the crush. Inside the station, there's Aqua Man and Wonder Woman, Thor with his Hammer, and the Valkyries with Shields, all bound for the comic convention.

As the boy searches for Molca by the tracks, he spots Speedy Gonzalez and a woman with painted tears carrying a doll. "*Arriba, arriba,*" calls the mouse, and the woman cries more. Maybe she's *La Llorona*, the Bawling Woman—Juanito isn't sure. Her children might be stolen or lost. Some people laugh at her but not him.

Fresh tamales steam somewhere, although peddlers are prohibited. A bootblack snaps a cloth by his kit, as he shines dusty Oxfords. The smell of the polish and food don't mix.

The boy ducks down by a commuter bench.

He spots Molca's boxing hightop shoes by the iron rails, on the boarding platform. James Hannity's glossy loafers and a man wearing scuffed huge wingtips have him cornered. People's legs scissor to and fro, a kelp forest brimming at neap tide. Juanito has his antennae out for Steve who still hasn't arrived.

The boy squeezes up close to his friend to do what he can.

"Just serve me the subpoena," Molca tells Hannity. "I'll be on my way."

"Sign this paper first," Hannity pokes his chest with a pen.

Molca tries to turn and walk. Hannity's big bodyguard blocks the path.

"Not so fast." Hannity grins and steps away from a surveillance camera so he won't be recorded.

"Hand me the summons, okay," Molca says, standing his ground. "I'm not looking for trouble. But no one's signing anything." Molca shows both hands and tries to exit.

Hannity pushes a tamale vendor out of his way to stop Steve, knocks loose the basket so that Señora Evermonde's wares fly everywhere. The boy knows the Señora because she's from Shelltown also. Travelers treat her as if she's not there.

Molca stoops to help pick up the spilled dozens. Lucky for her, the husks are wrapped in tin foil.

Juanito runs up to tell Molca that Doc's in bad shape.

Just then Lyle Carson pushes through the crowd and grabs the flyweight from behind.

"*Mi amor,*" Molca says over his shoulder.

Juanito laughs because his champion's counterpunching, *Slide, glide, and tenderize.* Lyle's wants him mad, so Molca makes fun instead of losing his temper.

Just then Steve dashes up from the shelter, red-faced and sweaty. "Enough," he says. "Come to your senses, everyone! Doc's had an emergency."

Doc's in the hospital, and Steve tries to lead Molca away past the thugs.

Lyle Carson cold cocks the minister, punches his face.

Señora Evermonde screeches and tosses her basket at Lyle. Molca's fists go up.

"No," Steve says and wipes his mouth. "Professor Carson's on camera. Let him explain." The minister waves on Molca and Juanito so that they leave right then. But the pastor and his charges don't reach the exit.

Señora Evermonde tells what happens this way. *Her full name is Zeta-Acosta, for the record.* After Lyle punches the padre in the face, Guzmán steps up to fight. But the pastor grabs Molca's arm and points to the surveillance camera. He won't let go. Molca tugs the pastor off balance yet can't throw a punch.

"Doc first," the pastor insists. "Let's hurry!"

Guzmán nods, eyes Lyle, and puts down his arms. He walks away and Steve catches up.

Juanito laughs and skips behind Steve and Guzmán. His friends are back—Doc will get better.

Lyle Carson eyes the kid, then backhands him hard. James Hannity slaps Guzmán with the summons and stuffs it in his shirt. The bodyguard laughs.

That's when the padre takes his cut shoulder out of the sling and knocks Lyle down. "Jesus Freak," Carson wheezes, grits his teeth and stands up, "That all you got?"

The parson slams him in the stomach. "Some Old Testament!" the minister shakes out his arm. The stitches from the Ashton Suites are leaking, his sleeve's wet. No matter, Carson's retching his guts.

That's when Hannity sneaks up and slugs Molca in the mouth.

Molca wipes the blood away. "*Bienvenidos*," Molca points, "Welcome to my world."

Now Senora Evermonde makes tamales from scratch. When the corn *masa* is ready for the pork filling, she gives each mound of dough a whack to lie flat. That's how the punches land. Hannity reels backward while throwing wild blows.

"*Una paliza mundial,*" she exults, a righteous whuppin'.

Hannity realizes that he better stay down.

But his bodyguard grabs Molca by the throat. Juanito, though, runs up to the fray, rips out the troll's back pocket and tosses his wallet on the tracks.

The big *cabron* curses and runs after his billfold. Señora Evermonde trips his double-X wingtip shoes, which scrapes his knee and shreds his pants.

"Thank you, Jesús," Señora Evermonde whoops, then puts a hand over her mouth. She strides up to Hannity in her flower dress and worn Keds and murmurs, "*pinche gavacho* bully."

And then she presses her earnings for the day into Molca's hand. "That's for the kids," she says in Spanglish. "Teach them like that!" she mimes a punch. How angry she's been and couldn't say it.

Juanito's never heard her talk that way. No one mouths back. The boy thanks her and takes the lead back to the shelter through his shortcuts.

28

IN THE MISSION'S dining hall, Rhoda carries two steaming plates of food to a mother and daughter who lost their farm a while back in the Kitchen Creek wildfire. Insurance for the lost property hasn't been settled or paid. They lost their income when their prize herd of goats perished. So they camp in their car.

"Smells wonderful," they inhale the aroma of the cooking. "How's Dr. Reese? We heard the ambulance."

"Doc went to the hospital," Rhoda says. "We're okay. Try the rhubarb cobbler." She wants not to lie.

Now Rhoda's been to funeral wakes in Shelltown where whole families honor the deceased, children, as well as the adults. Everyone takes their turn filing past the funeral bier. Also, the barrio celebrates the Day of the Dead, *el día de los muertos,* when for twenty-four hours families invite the departed back home to eat and rest. Marigolds and candles line the steps to the relatives' makeshift altars.

Death haunts Rhoda because of her mother's inoperable cancer. And now Doc's gone first.

Doc made her promise to see him buried, swear an oath—and not just Rhoda. But no last rites are set for the old man as they are for Thelma's memorial service. A location for a grave haunts Rhoda, especially, a resting place. And she wonders, I have a spot for him. Is that choice only in my head? Would we be wrong to dare? Doc belongs at the Settlement, We all agree. The gym, the infirmary, his spirit is here. Though he's a veteran, he's refused a military cemetery, and there are no next of kin. Just us.

The boy Juanito's by himself this minute watching over Doc. The police aren't involved in a search because the community hospital didn't report Doc missing. *Yet what about the brawl at the trolley? Bad publicity is poison, especially this moment. The authorities could launch an investigation.*

Across from the dining table, at the warming counter, Steve replenishes the simmering mulligan stew from a five-quart pot. He glances at Rhoda, since he just overheard the inquiry about Doc from the homeless women. The cast-iron kettle requires both hands as he refills the stainless server.

Dinner proceeds as it does each evening, which is the plan while they decide about Doc. Steve and Rhoda stay busy in the serving line, like every Tuesday. Molca supervises in the kitchen. The residents are seated first. Then hungry pop-ups from the queue outside go next. Tonight, there won't be any leftovers.

Earlier that day, as Doc was rushed to the emergency room by ambulance, Rhoda made up a name Raúl Ruiz because Manny hides his identity in public. She claimed to be his sister, Rosa. There was little time in the hospital for paperwork right then. An ER nurse asked "Rosa" to wait in the lobby, which Rhoda did—for hours it seemed.

She tried to find out Doc's condition, but the staff put her off. Steve didn't answer his phone, so she left a message to call her. Guzmán didn't pick up his cell either, which told her that there was trouble at the trolley station.

She imagined that the worst had occurred. Was there a fight on the platform? Had Juanito been injured? Was she wrong for sending a kid? But why should he watch his coach and friend die, his *maestro of wings*?

At the hospital, a patient somewhere in the ward was yelling, out of his head. An alarm sounded, short blats on the intercom. Then a "code blue" was called in the trauma bay. More staff rushed there.

Rhoda snuck through the emergency room door. Curtains were drawn around a cubicle nearby—she parted the fabric and entered. A sheet covered Doc, the heart monitor was off. No one had paged "Rosa Ruiz." Intravenous lines dangled from the bedside poles, slow drops wet the floor.

Rhoda has excavated the interred bones of people and their buried remains. Anthropology is her profession, cultures living and dead. Yet what training blunts grief—brainwork's not death.

"Hell, he just bit me," an attendant yelled from another area. The commotion registered barely with Doc right there. Manny had never wanted last rites; her mother either.

The disinfectant fumes and the hospital smell made her grab hold of a bed rail.

"Are you all right?" someone asked.

Her first thought was Doc and the oath she'd made. How was she supposed to comply? "I need a moment alone," she requested, which was

WORDS UNSPOKEN, THINGS UNSEEN

true and not accurate, not quite. Maybe Steve and Molca had a solution. They needed to hurry before the authorities stepped in.

The nurse brought in a chair and left. Rhoda and Doc were in the cubicle.

Why compel me to do the impossible? she seethed at him. *You know the college where I work! They want me to retire, so I can't take risks. The administration expects research to turn a profit, which makes my field second-class. Lyle plagiarized my book and got away with it.*

You, Doctor, you were cashiered for speaking your conscience, while you had to hide because you preferred men. Yet whether your name is Ruiz or Reese, you're still a physician. You had to live underground because of your orientation, but you keep the title MD even unto death. What about "Rosa"? How can you champion the underdog and overlook her? Her coffin comes in pink, and so will mine. She's not made up.

Rhoda had sworn to bury Dr. Manfred Saul Reese, not put him to rest. Who had claimed that brainwork's not death? So flat an assertion isn't science!

Someone put a hand on Rhoda's shoulder, which she shrugged off. When she turned around, Steve was there.

"I'm sorry," he said, lowering his voice, closing the curtains tight. "There's no time to mourn. We have to move him and decide what to do."

The authorities would step in, which was why Steve had put on a clerical collar to take charge and brought a wheelchair. His cut arm was not in a sling. But it hadn't healed—a trickle of blood marred a cuff. And his nose and jaw were bruised and swollen.

"What about Juanito?" she asked.

"The boy's at the shelter. We figured the worst. And Molca's waiting in the car, by the way. We decided that was smart," the minister murmured. "What with his scars and his looks, security might stop us."

Like "Rosa," she thought to herself.

"We drove fast as we could," the pastor handed her Manny's tan fedora. Then Steve retrieved a velcro neck brace from a surgical table and placed it on Manny.

The minister lifted Doc to the wheel chair and fit his hat. The old man weighed nothing, and the brim slipped over his forehead

"All right," Steve murmured, gripping the handles, "A tomb is my strength."

Rhoda froze for a second. Either she was in or out, no matter the consequences. Forget heaven or hell. She removed her scarf and draped it around Doc's neck.

The two of them wheeled Manny to the car through all the closed doors, their eyes front. Rhoda expected alarms to go off. When a guard appeared at the exit, Steve pointed to his cleric's collar, as if Manny was asleep and his pastor was in charge.

No one said stop.

Just as they reached the car, Molca carried Manny to the passenger's seat. She fastened Doc's seatbelt, although she felt absurd, almost laughed. Farce this was, a comic hearse from a bad film. Then she recalled Juanito's expression when the ambulance came.

"Old man, we'll get you home somehow," she said out loud. Molca started the engine and added, "We'll figure it out."

During the drive, no one talked.

At the mission shelter, they parked and waited a moment to let the blood settle. Molca checked the rear mirror before cracking his door. The dusk smelled of tailpipes and ocean. They wheeled Doc to the manse. On the way, while she steadied one shoulder, people cleared a path—that she remembers.

"Just returned from the hospital," Molca told the residents, "We're okay. He's with us." That wasn't a lie.

And back in the shelter cafeteria, Rhoda serves residents as if nothing's wrong, while only a few feet away in the rectory, the boy's alone with Doc. The three adults have to follow routine as if everything's normal. How else can they decide how to bury Doc without giving themselves away? So they pleaded with the boy, "Please go home, Juanito. You can't stay."

"He's my friend too," the boy had insisted. "I won't go away; I'm not just a kid. There's nowhere else. I'm not scared."

The other day at the Harrington exhibit, Rhoda had an inkling that ghosts haunt the mission.

"Hello, Lily," a voice broke in. *Actually, a wraith spoke, but that's not how she felt.* Were the doors locked? Were there guards outside? She thought she was safe.

There Lyle was.

"Professor Bart," he challenged, "I know you won't reconcile. So here's a proposition: We all do wrong, but who else we got besides each other?"

Being ourselves didn't settle anything, she told herself. A bad match sets a jinx. Scarabs dine better than we did with each other.

"Cut the shit, kiddo," Lyle fired back. "Why not choose me? Where's your unsealed curiosity, your method of doubt? The variables too messy, the uncertainty?"

You're like Harrington, muses Rhoda as she clears dinner plates in the cafeteria. Thin through the soul, no matter how smart. Good intentions don't program like math.

Rhoda stands by the pantry, listening.

Harrington's ex-wife Carobeth mentions his terror of death, of not being able to think, of being erased. Harrington begs her to run over his legs if he's ever drafted for war. Being crippled for life is preferable to dying in battle, no longer able to reason. Why then did Harrington lock up his heart? she wonders. Will Juanito recover after this disaster? His mentor and friend is gone. Is a child able to come to terms with death, especially Doc's?

And Rhoda wonders whether clarity is a gift, no matter how hard it is to see what's in front of us. If we recognize the wrong people, we can get out of the way—learn to escape. But death is inevitable.

She carries a plate of stew to a student who can't afford rent and sleeps under a bridge. She tries not to stare.

29

THE GHOSTY OL' owl perched on the roof smells fresh corn bread right out of the oven and hot stew from the stove.

Doc Manny must be hungry. Juanito glances over at his coach. *I'll fetch something for dinner.*

But Manny won't wake up ever. You know that! Why pretend you don't get it?

And Juanito recalls why he's here with Doc: there's no other family except us. But he shouldn't be at the shelter. The police might come. Everything has to stay quiet, as if nothing's wrong. Which is why the grown-ups are at the cafeteria serving dinner as usual.

Though Padre Steve, Rhoda, and Molca were just in the rectory with Doc and him, they had to carry on like normal. Before they left him alone, the boy recalls the padre pacing back and forth by Doc's wheelchair. "What about Juanito?" the parson wondered out loud. "A child shouldn't suffer for us."

Then Juanito spoke up, "I'm not just a kid. I've been listening!"

Molca turned to the minister and tapped his own head. "You, Rhoda, and me brought Doc here. What now, send the kid to bed? He's past making himself small. Let's do as we promised!"

And Molca smoothed Doc's wool blanket and said, "We'll figure a way, old man."

"What of the shelter, all these people?" snapped the padre. "Not only us four."

"When I turned pro and won my first fight," Molca offers, "Doc took me to a steakhouse by the harbor, a famous place; no shorts or flip-flops permitted.

Molca's telling this story on purpose, not just to reminisce. "There was filet mignon that thick or wild halibut broiled with dill butter. Fresh oysters on the shell, a rack of lamb. But I wanted a burger."

"'That's not on the menu,' Doc advised. 'Let's grind up the waiter.'"

Juanito laughs but wipes his eyes. He's heard the story.

"Doc stood up to leave the restaurant," Molca shows the kid. "So I reminded him, 'You made reservations for dinner. They expect us to eat.'"

"'Today you fought smart,' Doc replied. 'No box-canyon logic, no mindless chatter. Instead of slugging toe-to-toe, you circled and jabbed. Knee-jerk thinking was out, reflex-mad on pause. Power didn't trap you. Let's celebrate!'"

"My dad tells me, 'Be a man,'" chimes in the boy.

"We have to unthink what's expected," replies Molca. "That's what Doc meant. Step up to point zero. If we do, we can figure out his send-off."

And though the boy's alone with Doc, he imagines Rhoda and Steve carrying plates of food to the residents like normal, with the smells and the steam.

An icy draft leaks under the door. Manny's so cold.

Outside, jets sink out of earshot as they land at the airport. The windows quit rattling, and the walls don't shake. Yet the boy's thoughts tilt out of plumb. Is there forgiveness for burying Doc? Or just that ghosty old owl nailed to the toolshed that scares away crows.

See, I told them I would be okay, that I'm not afraid Juanito thinks and squeezes the old man's hand. Don't think bad thoughts and erase him. Hold on to the good.

What does it mean just to end? Juanito wonders. To give up one's pulse and go silent. No eyes, no voice, no attention. If the spirit returns to God when we pass from this world, what remains of a person? Is breath all that's human, the body just a house. Who we were vanishes, what we felt. Does the strike of a bell ever vanish, fall away from the source? Or does it ripple the air always, unheard?

And Juanito realizes, my father is dead to me, though Doc's the one who has passed on. Silvio smashes the calm whenever he shows up drunk. So he's death. I can't help how I feel. He's my father, yet I'm ashamed, which is like a grave. Someday, maybe, will I be able to love him?

Rhoda's Chimayó blanket covers Doc like a cloak. And the boy tells himself, *He's asleep. As long as we're here, he's with us!*

A mockingbird sings blind. Everyone's at the kitchen tables across the way, in the cafeteria, that's why the chirping's so loud.

Evening settles like fog.

In the parson's rectory, as the wind-spurred jacaranda scrapes the glass, Juanito tries to whistle like a finch. The boy purses his lips and wonders, *perhaps Manny's soul wanders the bay already, since he was a sailor.*

Again the salt breeze stutters; dinner's being served!

I'll bring Manny a steaming bowl of stew and rice, muses the boy. Opportunity stew, some folk call it, joking about luck. As if the meat owes to God. The vegetables we plant right here.

Nothing's sure unless we grow it from seed. We protect the plants from the bugs and the wind.

Nails carom in a rusty bucket, such are the boy's thoughts. There's a hole in his mind. In the barrio, there are wakes for the dead with the viewing and rosary. For cousin Angelita, his age, who died from her tonsils during the anesthesia. And his *tio* Cuco, his uncle from the army, who blew up on patrol. *Though the caskets are scary, we show our respect.* That's why Juanito's family celebrates *el dia de los muertos* with the skeleton bread.

Doc's asleep in the corner. His hat and Rhoda's scarf muffle him up, while the sea wind scratches outside.

The grown-ups and I stand watch, the boy muses, *though they're not here. They want me to be okay by myself, so they can be all right.*

Maybe I'm asleep, wonders the boy. *Dreaming. Under the bedcovers.* Except, outside the window, a nighthawk swoops up moths by the street lamps. Or is it a bat? Wings dive and bank, shadows flicker. The dark is real.

I'll fetch Doc a cool glass of jamaica from dried hibiscus flowers, his favorite drink.

But Manny's gone, remember. The dry fountain's for him. Once it's bolted down on the cofferdam plinth, Molca can hook up the plumbing. And the boy imagines water cascading down the bronze fountain bowls, sheets of bubbles and spume. *Close by the birds, right next to the garden, Doc Manny's not lonely. He can rest.*

And Juanito smoothes the Chimayó blanket because silence is what Manny wants.

30

MEANWHILE, AS SUPPER winds down in the shelter's cafeteria, the minister's haunted by a headstone. The pastor's confirmed with the county hospital that the Settlement's made the final arrangements for Dr. Reese, which the shelter's done before for other residents. This time, however, he prays that God shows the way.

Juanito's alone with Doc Manny.

Just a few weeks ago the padre recalls, Doc had commandeered him, a pastor, to come with Doc to Saint Joan's Hospice in the valley nearby. The commander asked Steve to drive because he couldn't. The pilgrimage was a favor for Rhoda's mom, Thelma, who wasn't strong enough to bid farewell to an old friend, Maureen, who refused more kidney dialysis. Maureen had asked her friends to visit one last time.

The parson, let it be said, fumed all the while. Here they were, Steve and the old man, paying their respects to a stranger. What about Doc, especially since a military burial was out of the question? The pastor sympathized with the old man's sense of betrayal. Yet what was the plan?

Saint Joan's hospice, for the record, is as welcoming a place as death allows. Maureen, Thelma's high-school classmate, asked the pastor to read from Nehemiah, "Do not be grieved, for the joy of the Lord is your strength."

The pastor glanced at the old man who claimed no religion, but whose dogtags were stamped *Jewish* because of his family's ancient Sephardic roots.

Pressed hard about what he believes, the physician calls himself a sheeny Buddhist, a Zen Semite. Medicine is his temple. Even then, says Siddharta, all phenomena are empty, the body included. Escaping the wheel of rebirth begins with stilling the body and mind. And yet Doc's cosmic "duh" about spiritual matters binds his friends like a creed. Profess what you will or you won't, consider how Doc honored a friend of a friend.

At Saint Joan's, the slow anguish of leavetaking tests everyone. Death at the mission is quick, mostly: drug overdoses, strokes, heart attacks. The worst *months are winter. Just weeks ago, however, when the flu struck early, two residents expired, one after the other*

"Poor dear, Thelma's friend, Maureen," mulled Steve after the hospice visit. "God forgive me, passing slow is a trial."

"You mean messy, don't you?" Doc corrected the preacher's euphemizing. "*In media res*," Doc offered in Latin, as he caught his breath on their way out of the facility. The pastor hadn't brought Manny's wheelchair, at his request. Doc, after all, was a soldier.

Manny's Latin phrase surprised the pastor because it was high church, and the language of the Spanish Inquisition that kicked out the jews. The expression *in medias res* translated as "into the midst of things." Into the crush of circumstance. And the pastor figured, Here comes another favor. Maureen's funeral probably. Which wasn't fair, because how could Steve say "no" to a dying man who was his friend.

Instead of Maureen, though, Doc switched to Rhoda who provides care for her mother. Rhoda's the person who prepares a hot lunch every day and gives her mom showers. Rhoda's the one who launders the soiled bed sheets and soaked night clothes.

Not Rhoda's sister Deirdre, a nurse practitioner, who lives in town also.

And the parson exclaimed, "Deirdre?" Why had she come up? Was her example some sort of Zen *koan*, an existential riddle? Deirdre wipes down everything with bleach when she drops by Thelma's house: bed frame, toilet, towel racks, even the door knobs. And then she goes away.

"Even the angels need rest," Doc told the parson. "Rhoda could use some help. I'd offer to drop by myself, but . . ." Doc tapped his wristwatch.

"No," Steve sighed, "That's not fair. There are caretakers and a nurse." And what about squiring you around the parson stewed quietly, shamed or not.

"The Knights of the Ordinary work a double shift," Doc Manny said. "Then it's ten percent more."

"What sort of math?" Steve groused, "One hundred and ten percent effort!"

"Even unto death," joshed Doc, who tapped Steve's shoulder. "I'm on call, remember," the old man smiled. The pastor's impatience felt puny and jacked.

What does God expect of me? the minister broods in the shelter kitchen. *The boy's alone with Doc, and heaven won't show the way.*

Steve's struck with how Manny's way of saying goodbye was tending to friends. That was the old man's requiem, the last act of kindness.

And the minister recalls Doc's memorial fountain. Even while under construction, that spot was his. There he belonged. The doctor loved the birds and the garden and being part of a crew.

Again the boy leaps to mind, who's with Doc.

31

"I'M NOT SAD," the kid says, "and I am." Juanito looks over at Doc who's seated upright in the wheelchair. "Manny was awful tired." The boy smoothes the Chimayó blanket that serves as Doc's cowl. The shell of a man is not what's there to him.

Silence crowds the narrow rectory where four pallbearers mind Doc's wake: the minister and Guzmán, Rhoda and Juanito.

The adults have returned from serving the residents dinner in the cafeteria. They're relieved that Juanito's okay and of mixed minds about letting him stay. They have to decide about Doc, on what to do next.

Molca wipes the window glass and checks the light.

Northeast, away from the city, faint stars wink over the mountains. The vague moon silvers skyscrapers; random clouds dapple their facades. Not far away from the mission, the homeless bed down where there's space on the sidewalks. No matter the direction, shadows seems to be flying apart, dis-aggregating, a slow-motion earthquake.

"Should we call the authorities?" observes the minister. "Do no harm," he quotes from Doc's Hippocratic oath, since the shelter will suffer if a dead man's not reported.

"No!" Juanito exclaims. "They'll come and take him. With us, he's here. By the garden he's not lonely."

"But he's gone and won't know," Molca tests the youngster.

"But we will," replies the boy who looks at each of the grown-ups.

"Remember the city council meeting about bulldozing the shelter," the youngster switches voices, "the one with the tuba. Doc went door to door to ask people to come. There was a crowd. The officials voted down the demolition, and there was an uproar. Some folk were happy; some were mad."

Molca thinks back and nods. The minister and Rhoda don't know what to say—the boy's opening up to them.

Juanito rubs his mouth and continues. "One row of people in the front yelled at Doc. They called him a 'queer.'"

"I laughed at him too," the boy admits. "It happened so fast. I stopped, but too late. Maybe he saw me? Calling names hurts. My father does it to me."

"Not just Silvio," Molca replies. "Me. I've got a bad habit of mouthing off."

"I told you I was in prison, right?" Guzmán faces the youngster.

"Youth Authority," replies the boy, "hardcorps punks, wanna-be gangsters."

"Marked kids, that's for sure," Molca ventures. "When I was in juvenile hall, Doc asked why I was there. 'Stabbed both my parents,' I told him, 'I'm 'incorrigible.''"

"'Incorrigible . . .'" Doc paused and glanced at me. "What does that mean?" Molca mimics Doc's explain-that-to-me face and points at the old man in the wheelchair.

"My parents disowned me, I told Doc. School threw me out. I was a lost cause.

"Know what he said?" Molca turns to the boy. "Change takes practice. I was too angry.

"Because of Doc, eventually I was released from that prison for juveniles," Guzmán muses. "Manny talked to my parents, pleaded with the court—became my guardian. And for all that good will, I branded him different, not man enough. I laughed at Doc just like you did."

"Quality's in the person, in time I figured that out. I never apologized though for my bigotry. I felt ashamed. But I donated blood for his transfusions and told him, 'Thanks, Coach. My turn.'"

"You're in college, now," Juanito says. "That's good, right?"

"Sometimes," Molca agrees. "Ideas are another country. Actually changing, crossing the border. That's hard. Though my roots span the globe, I shadow box in a corner. How do I unthink the narrows?" Molca raises his gloves to his chest.

Juanito recalls walking to Franklin Elementary School. On the way to the school, by Chicano Park, there's a flock of swarming glossy-winged grackles crowding and thinning in many shapes. The word "murmuration" comes from Rhoda who's seen the flock. At school, there are bullies. No one's safe. Not the students, not the teachers. Without a safe place, he can't fit. His mind slips off math and reading.

"I know why Manny started a boxing school," the boy speaks up, He throws a make-believe punch and puts on Doc's voice, "Let's lead the future with a jab," The kid dances a little footwork and says, "Make aggression smart!"

"Let's turn some lives around," Molca choruses. "Stay heads up."

Guzmán bows, as if to a tough opponent. "Doc's speciality is engineering comebacks . . . was," he pauses. "Those longshots include us. Let's do what's right!"

"I'm losing my mother," Rhoda sighs, looking out at the Seven Sisters where Venus crosses them in the sky.

"The shelter's at risk," the minister reminds everyone. "And we could go to jail if we're caught."

"I've done time," Guzmán advises. "Sometimes outside is worse."

"God help me; I'm responsible for these people," replies the minister.

"Us too," Molca says and rolls down his sleeves.

"Let's honor him and not make a scandal," Rhoda interrupts, glancing at Doc. And then she searches their faces. "The memorial fountain fits over the pit of the caisson like a capstone, air tight and locked. Let's plumb it true and settle him there in that protected space. He did right by us!"

The boy bites his lip and glances around, as if they forgot that he's there.

"We gave our word," Guzmán affirms.

"The gantry hoist that lifts the fountain, where is it?" Rhoda asks.

"Right by the cofferdam," replies Molca. "It's there by the concrete hull, ready to go, no matter the lift."

"Wait," the minister holds up his hand. "Let me pray on it."

"Til Judgment Day," Molca tells him. "Guilt lasts longer."

"Half right," mulls the pastor checking his watch, "We have to lock up the shelter at ten."

"Amen," says Rhoda, "Go on you two, Put the shelter to sleep. Decide by then. Juanito and I will stand watch."

32

AT TEN IN the evening, 2200 hours by military time, Molca and the padre regroup in the pantry workroom, as required, in order to cross-check tomorrow's schedule and their lists of to-dos. The parson reviews timesheets, audits bills, receipts, and inventories supplies—despite all that's happened, there's work. More homeless are crowding the shelter because of the comic convention and its legions of tourists. For appearance's sake, the police corral vagrants and move them along. Many appear at the gate.

While the minister tends to the paperwork, Molca checks the cafeteria which is overdue for an inspection by the Board of Health. With the serving lines closed, the food-handling areas are being steam-cleaned from top to bottom. The walls and floors follow. With that job in progress, Guzmán inspects the kitchen, under the bank of stoves, especially, and all through the stainless steel counters and sinks. The he doublechecks the temperatures in the chill room and the freezer.

After Steve and Molca complete their tasks, the two walk through the dorms bidding the residents good night, and they assist security as the staff secures the grounds and locks up.

Finally, the nightwatch sets the fire alarms. An all-clear is broadcast via radio. Then the hour gives over to sleep.

For the minister, stopping at the chapel is vital, no matter the hour. Molca stands by the door.

From under the vacant folding chairs inside the sanctuary, the pastor retrieves a stray wrapper for nicotine gum and an empty styrofoam coffee cup. Then he stays on knees. "Into your hands . . . ," he prays.

It's not just Doc's burial that weighs on the minister—it is also breaking the law. What about living true to the gospel? How does God judge what's done in his name? Strictly by the commandments, by good deeds, by the quality of our character despite flaws?

The padre's vexed also about the trolley station brawl. Bad press spells disaster right now. He should have reined in his temper.

Guzmán finally enters the chapel and retrieves him. "Sorry, Padre," his right-hand murmurs, "The others are waiting. It's late."

As they walk back in silence to the rectory, Molca wonders out loud, "Going to court over those secret tests shook him, especially when a judge shut out his testimony. They let me fight in the ring, but not him," Guzmán marvels. "And a lot more's at stake than boxing."

"So what's to be done, Guzmán?" queries the minister. "The military will lay him under a field of crosses. That's not for Manny the Hat!

"Either is a poor man's grave in a potter's field, care of the city! What a turn for a Knight of the Ordinary, that's who he was!"

To the minister's mind, the angels inspired the gym and the outpatient clinic. Even with a project as green as a garden, the old man battled the politicians. A fountain grows out of concrete despite the downtown traffic. How could God not have a hand?

You in grace, Guzmán?" the padre asks his right hand. "Time for Doc's send-off. Let's do right by our Knight."

"Heaven's far," Molca answers.

33

SECRETS EMBARK ON cloudy nights when the dark fronts the passage. Four conspirators spirit Doc to Rhoda's room and make ready to pipe him to rest under the fountain.

Once at her lab, the professor gathers three coffee mugs from a cupboard and a bottle of brandy from a handwoven basket. She pours three shots at her desk, then retrieves a glass of *jamaica* for Juanito.

"To Doc," she toasts and the four raise their glasses.

Molca takes the lead bathing Doc and washes his hair. One person alone can lift him; two manage the weight. The boy retrieves Doc's fine suit of combed Vicuña wool, dark ocean blue, and grooms the nap with a boar-bristle brush. Guzmán dusts Manny's classic Borsalino felt hat and shapes it by hand. The men dress him article by article, like a warrior. Elegant silk tie knotted in place, birthstone cufflinks, engraved silver wristwatch, fine polished wingtips—Dr. Manfred Saul Reese, Lieutenant Commander, retired, ready to be escorted ashore.

"Let's put him back in the wheelchair," Molca says.

The minister and Guzmán each take an arm. But the seat tips back and Doc strikes his head.

"We didn't mean it," gasps the boy. He won't let Manny's face be covered.

"Ahoy, Dr. Reese, where away?" Rhoda steps forward.

"Fair wind," the pastor points at a window; Branches scrape against the glass. "Set the sails."

Molca retrieves the Chimayó blanket and tells Manny, "We're on the tide, Commander."

The minister lays his hand on Doc Manny's brow. "Physician, healer, friend," he utters.

Molca arranges the cowl but not like a shroud. The ship's physician fought mute obedience. Distinction suits a rebel.

"Lifting the fountain requires a team," Guzmán cautions. "In the dark, especially, it's dangerous. We need to be careful."

"That's you and me," Rhoda answers. "We'll go outside and check the footing right now. We'll decide how to heft the weight."

"I'm not just a kid," Juanito says.

Rhoda nods.

"Wait," objects the minister, "Don't leave me out."

"The residents come first," she answers. "A hundred need you."

"This isn't a classroom," the priest grouses. "Don't lecture."

On a new moon, before sunrise, the four of them bury Manny in the cofferdam hull near the garden and use the heavy fountain for his gravestone.

Molca goes alone first to scout the site by himself. "Let me reconnoitre the grounds," he insists. "I'll dial from my cell if anything goes bad."

Eyes are watching at a shelter, even after curfew.

Repairs at the mission, though, occur day or night. There's no need to hide if they set out a task. Guzmán sets up halogen worklights, a tripod of bulbs, and checks the gantry hoist's freeplay to test the rig. The lifting chains slide freely through the cadmium-plated pulleys. The heavy fountain will seal the cofferdam, a capstone that defeats detection.

Then, after Guzmán dials the crew from his mobile phone, Rhoda appears, which is not unusual since site-archeologists inspect projects at all hours. She and Molca attach the rigging that lifts the fountain. Any resident would grump at the late hour, curse that it's business as usual, and try to go back to sleep.

The four pallbearers outside have to keep moving, no matter the clamor. Rhoda and Guzmán clear dirt from around the concrete lip of the hull, despite the thud and jar of the shovels. They position the bulky steel mats for the A-frame's wheels. Hemp cordage muffles the block and tackle. Chocks and shims are ready for the heavy lift. Next, they clear a path for the wheelbarrows. Cobblestones are in a mound for ballast, loose sand is piled up for fill.

There's no talk, except for safety's sake. They stop to rest at intervals, few as possible.

Lieutenant Commander Reese will rest on a knoll, tucked up like a fetus. Even as a rising sea claims the plot, he will stand clear.

Once the site is prepared for the lift, the halogen glare is turned down. Night sounds rise up; their vision returns. They dab at the sweat and fog. Juanito wipes his eyes as if from the work.

The reinforced concrete box is ready for the memorial fountain. The rectory's not far. The plan is to wheel Doc Manny to the caisson, the four of them.

The wind switches direction and gusts from the bay. The cool chills their sweat. As fog sets in, moist fingers damp the nightshine. Another Santa Ana will ignite tomorrow.

"Wait," the priest cautions after they reach the manse, "five people go out from here, four and an empty wheelchair can't come back."

"Let me go first," volunteers the boy. "No one notices a stray. I'll ride back so the count evens. You push." The boy leaves.

After a few minutes, the adults bring Doc.

Steve and Molca leap into the pit and lay down a bier of sheepskin, the soft wool padding from the shelter's infirmary.

Rhoda and the boy hand down Doc Manny, wrapped in his Chimayó shroud. Branches of thyme and sage and wild fennel serve as his bed, since Juanito already has prepared the resting place. After Steve and Molca climb out of the pit, Juanito casts down fresh larkspur blossoms and cosmos flowers that he gathered from the garden.

"Doc was a sailor," Molca says, scattering the first shovelful of earth over his friend. The rattling fill unnerves him. "Doc Manny was a sailor," he repeats, "embarking aboard ship, changing vessels—always arriving. He was mestizo too, although the borders are different. He showed me kindness despite my closed mind. Hope, sometimes, is under construction. Doc proved it."

"I remember happy moments," the boy offers. "we planted the garden!" He closes his eyes and tosses a fistful of soil. "Recollecting the good makes people better. Doc believed that."

Rhoda takes up the spade and muses, "My mom and he shared poetry, read out loud. Which is more than the sounds of words, but beauty in action."

"May there be abundant peace from heaven," the reverend goes last, praying the Kaddish at dawn, "healing, redemption, forgiveness, atonement." And he adds, "our's, not just this man."

The four conspirators chorus, "Amen."

"Don't worry, Juanito, he's with us," Rhoda offers, sprinkling more flowers.

"I keep him close," the boy sighs.

Manny's covered with earth, finally; and they make ready to haul up the fountain and cap his grave. Just then the hoist chains snag. And when they free the links, the pulleys won't grab the weight and lift the sculpture into place.

The reverend glances at the sky and mutters, "No jokes, please!"

Molca reaches for his flashlight. "The fountain's not level," he informs them. "One corner sunk in the dirt. It's stuck."

"What do we do?" asks the boy.

"Move that corner to firm ground, over a half foot, twelve centimeters, maybe. Try the hoist then."

"Lord willing," the minister says, "There's a thousand pounds, at least."

"Look East," points Rhoda. Sure enough, daybreak's at hand.

"Now or never," Guzmán says. "The padre and I lift the sag end, Rhoda and Juanito the side opposite."

The four of them together lean into the behemoth. "Only inches to go," they encourage each other. "One, two, three, lift . . . !"

Nothing happens.

"What are we, congress?" hisses the padre. "Haul up the anchor! Set the man free!"

Huffing and sweating, dawn at their backs, they try once, twice, three times. On their final effort, the four fall into synch. The weight of steel, aluminum and brass creaks and shifts, skids out of the low muddy trough.

The hoist chains run free so that they're able to inch the fountain over the cofferdam. As everyone stands clear, the four of them lower the bulk over the locking flange of concrete, and it snaps into place.

The boy whistles soft as a thrush.

No one speaks. A cactus wren, chatting and bold, greets the sun from an ocotillo bush.

The boy points at the sound, "Doc planted that rain cactus, thorns and all, from a dead branch. Look at it now!" Juanito's relieved, as if he's done nothing wrong. "Listen! DO you hear the song?"

EPILOG

The Photograph

AT THE SETTLEMENT rescue mission downtown, in the rectory of Pastor Stephen Robert Bentham, a group portrait hangs behind his desk. The outdoor photograph features the newly dedicated memorial fountain near the shelter's truck garden. The bronze plaque reads, **Dr. Manfred Saul Reese: Physician, Healer, Friend.**

Below the dedication, bees dot the flowers.

In the picture, Padre Steve's flanked by Rhoda and Molca. Juanito's in front.

Rhoda and Steve lean toward each other, almost touching, like parallel lines that never meet. Except for their smiles, which match. At least that's how the photograph's composed.

Guzmán's wearing a T-shirt with the boxing team's logo. The boy's turned toward him as if about to speak.

What the boy can't reveal to anyone is a message that he's left with Manny in the cofferdam hull. Laser-printed on cotton paper, size 14 font, folded in a plain envelope and tucked into a boxing glove that's placed beside him. *This is our friend Doc Manny. His heart gave out. He's here, and we won't forget him. The other's with me. That's all.*